THE POISONED PEER

A Churchill & Pemberley Mystery Book 6

EMILY ORGAN

The Poisoned Peer

Emily Organ

Chapter 1

"I ADORE iced fancies but they have one drawback," proclaimed Mrs Churchill to her assistant, Miss Pemberley, as they sat in a corner of the tea rooms.

"And what may that be?"

"They're too small." Churchill wiped her mouth with her serviette. "Shall we order another plateful?"

"Not for me thank you, I'm quite full up."

"How so? They barely touched the sides!"

"I only have a small stomach."

"Not much smaller than…" Churchill glanced down at her large bosom and decided against continuing the subject. "They've changed the tablecloths in here," she commented, glancing around at the pink gingham. "And the new curtains are pretty." The floral drapes in the bow window were patterned in pale blue and pink.

"By all means order another plate of iced fancies, Mrs Churchill, don't let me stop you," said Pemberley, "but I shall take myself off for a walk, it's a lovely afternoon." She brushed the crumbs off her plate onto the floor where her scruffy little dog, Oswald, enthusiastically licked them up.

Churchill glanced at her own empty plate, then at the sunny high street beyond the window.

"I suppose you're right, Pembers, conventional wisdom would dictate that a stroll in the outdoors is better for the body and mind than a second plate of cakes. I can't say I fully agree with that but I suppose there's no harm in moving about a bit." She summoned the waitress to pay for the bill.

"Shall we take the long route back to the office?" suggested Pemberley as the two ladies stepped out onto the cobbled high street with Oswald at their heels.

"What's wrong with the short route? I've just eaten all those iced fancies."

"You told me they didn't touch the sides."

"They didn't. But they're sitting rather heavily at the bottom. How long is the long route, exactly?"

"Just to the top of the high street and then down onto the riverside path, it will bring us out at the bottom of the high street and we can walk up from there to the office."

"It's not called the long route for nothing then."

"It won't take more than fifteen minutes, Mrs Churchill. You'll feel like you've had a proper trek once you've done it."

"Well if you insist. It will give me a chance to tell you about my new friend."

"Do you need a new one?"

"No, I don't *need* one. I have plenty of friends already but there's always room for more."

"And who is it?"

"Tryphena Ridley-Balls. We have a great deal in common."

"Oh, the Ridley-Balls."

"You've heard of them?"

"Yes, they own Gripedown Hall. The estate is enormous."

"Tryphena doesn't like to brag about it."

"But she's clearly mentioned it to you."

"She has, but only in the most discreet tones. The upper-classes don't like to boast."

"Her father must be the Earl of Middlemop then."

"He certainly is. Old aristocracy too, not one of those new-fangled Earls who made his fortune from liver pills or jam or something or other."

"He must be getting on a bit."

"Tryphena tells me that he's ninety-nine years of age."

"What an achievement."

"It is rather, isn't it?"

"I'm sure I heard somewhere that he's the richest man in Dorset."

"Wessex, actually."

"Tryphena told you that?"

"Yes, but she wasn't boasting. It was merely mentioned in passing."

"It sounds very much like boasting to me, I don't know how someone manages to slip into the conversation that their father is the richest man in Wessex without boasting."

"Well, when you meet Tryphena, you'll understand how. She's extremely modest."

"Will I *have* to meet her?"

"She's a good friend of mine, Pembers, the likelihood of your paths crossing is rather high."

"Oh."

"Don't look so downcast, you'll adore her. She's what I'd describe as the 'life and soul'."

"I'm not very good with people who are the life and soul. They're often tiresome."

"There is nothing tiresome about Tryphena, Pembers. Like you, she's never married so you'll have a lot in common."

"Because we've never married?"

"She is a wonderful creature."

"Oswald's a wonderful creature." She paused to watch him sniff at a bicycle propped up outside the pharmacy.

"Yes he is," agreed Churchill. The two ladies continued on their way.

"I prefer animals to people," said Pemberley.

"Well animals are rather lovely, but you can't have a conversation with them."

"I disagree."

Churchill resisted the urge to argue. "Well, back to Tryphena Ridley-Balls. I met her in that pleasant ladies' outfitters in Dorchester, the one by the pricey jewellers. I was in there browsing the skirts when I overheard a well-spoken voice asking a shop assistant about Harris tweed. At that very moment I knew that she was my sort of person and I inserted myself into the conversation."

"Because of the Harris tweed?"

"Of course! You know that I'm never seen out of it."

"Did you mention the Outer Hebrides by any chance?"

"Naturally."

"And you said that what was good enough for the Other Hebrideans was good enough for you."

"That's right, Pembers! Are you sure you weren't there yourself?"

"Quite sure."

"Oh dear, I do hope that my conversation isn't that

4

predictable. I worry now that I repeat myself a little too much. It's a sign of someone who's under-educated isn't it? They fail to furnish their brains with new information and instead merely repeat the same old stories. I'm concerned now that I'm the same. That doesn't bode well for my friendship with Tryphena, she'll soon tire of it."

"Only Tryphena?"

"What do you mean?"

"Oh look at that!" exclaimed Pemberley, pointing to their right. "A new shop!"

The two ladies stopped by the store which was painted a pleasing shade of lavender. Churchill felt an uncomfortable twinge as she observed the sewing machines in the window. Alongside them sat a well-arranged display of colourful ribbons, buttons, cotton reels and pretty pin cushions.

"Oh goodness, do you see what sort of shop this is, Pembers?"

"A sewing shop," said Pemberley.

"Not just a sewing shop. A haberdasher's!"

"Just like Mrs Thonnings' shop."

"Exactly like Mrs Thonnings' shop! But do we need another haberdashery here in Compton Poppleford? I can't imagine there would be enough customers. Oh golly, I wonder what Mrs Thonnings makes of it all."

Churchill thought of her friend and shook her head in lamentation, Mrs Thonnings' shop seemed decidedly tired and shabby when compared to the attractive emporium which sat before them.

A large lady with a head of thick, golden hair stepped out of the doorway. She wore scarlet lipstick and a matching scarlet scarf.

"You two ladies can't resist a browse I see!" Her voice was loud and cheery.

"Good morning," said Churchill. "I don't believe we've met. I'm Mrs Churchill and this is Miss Pemberley."

"Good morning ladies, I'm Mrs Bouton and I've brought buttons and bows to Compton Poppleford!"

"So I see." Churchill glanced up at the name of the shop and saw that it was elegantly named 'Boutons et Rubans'. "Are you aware there's already a shop selling buttons and bows?" she asked.

"Oh yes, that old place in the middle of the high street. Been there years I hear. Terribly old-fashioned."

"It belongs to our good friend Mrs Thonnings."

"Does it indeed? Well please don't take offence, Mrs Churchill, I'm merely stating my opinion."

"I think Mrs Thonnings would be terribly offended if she heard your opinion."

"I'm sure she would but the place is out-of-date, I maintain that whether or not she's your friend, Mrs Churchill. Your friend can refresh and update it of course, there's nothing preventing her from doing that."

"I imagine not. Have you lived in Compton Poppleford long?"

"No, not long. A few weeks. Everyone here seems perfectly delightful."

"They are, on the whole. Although they may be less than delightful if they hear you calling them old-fashioned."

"I call a spade a spade, Mrs Churchill. People will soon learn that about me."

Chapter 2

"WHAT AN ABRASIVE LADY," commented Pemberley as the two ladies continued on their way to the riverside path. They reached a row of little cottages with flowers blooming in window boxes. "I can't imagine her making many friends in the village."

"I don't think she's here to make friends, Pembers. She's clearly a lady of business. People aren't interested in friendships when they're being business-like. Now whatever you do, don't mention the new haberdashery shop to Mrs Thonnings."

"Surely she's seen it?"

"We don't know whether she has or not. If she hasn't then I certainly don't want to be the one breaking the news to her, it will result in a terrible outpouring of anguish and upset. You've seen how much nicer Mrs Bouton's shop is than Mrs Thonnings' place, it even has a fancy French name. Quite pretentious if you ask me, but it will certainly attract the aspirational customer. People are often drawn to places with French names in an attempt to appear sophisticated, don't you find? Anyway, we must remain shtum on

7

the matter when we next see Mrs Thonnings, just in case she isn't aware of the new shop yet."

"Well here she is now."

"Oh golly really?"

A red-haired lady in a floral tea dress was heading towards them from the riverside path. Oswald ran up to greet her and she made a fuss of him before approaching the two ladies.

"Oh good afternoon, Mrs Thonnings! How are you?"

She gave a sigh. "A little disgruntled, I'm afraid."

"Good, well that's nice. We're just—"

"Why is it nice that I'm disgruntled?"

"Oh, I do apologise. I'm sorry to hear it."

Churchill braced herself for the inevitable outpour of woe about the new haberdashery shop.

"Tiddles has begun scratching the legs of my dining table," said Mrs Thonnings.

"Oh, is that all?"

"What do you mean, *is that all*? The dining table belonged to my mother. It's an heirloom."

"I'm sorry to hear it. Cats can be so awfully naughty sometimes can't they?" Thoughts of pets made her glance at Oswald who was chewing flowers in a pot by a cottage door.

"Oh, Miss Pemberley! Get that dog under control. He really is a rascal."

"Those are Mrs Strawpost's nasturtiums," said Mrs Thonnings. "She'll be terribly annoyed about that."

"I'm sure she will," responded Churchill, watching her assistant pick up the wayward dog. "Pets eh, Mrs Thonnings? Destructive little beasts."

"But we love them all the same."

"Indeed we do, although I do wonder why sometimes. Anyway, try a coat of shoe polish on those table leg scratches, that should reduce their appearance a little. Hopefully all will be well."

"Thank you, I shall try that, Mrs Churchill."

"Good, well it's nice to have the problem solved then. Come along, Miss Pemberley, we must get back to the office. We have plenty of work to be getting on with."

"Do we?"

"Yes."

"Such as what?"

"Let's discuss it back at the office."

"And I'm quite annoyed about the new haberdasher's shop too," added Mrs Thonnings.

"Oh?"

"Have you seen it?"

"Yes, actually we have. But I wouldn't worry about it, Mrs Thonnings, I'm quite sure that Mrs Bouton poses no threat to your business."

"Well that's what I've decided too."

"Really?"

"I've decided to be sanguine and laissez faire about the matter. I have many loyal customers and I don't see why they should all suddenly defect to Mrs Fancy-Pants' new shop."

"Well she does have a rather nice window display," said Pemberley. "And some very pretty little pin cushions which—"

"Yes, thank you Miss Pemberley," interjected Churchill. "Mrs Thonnings doesn't wish to hear about it."

"Oh I couldn't care either way," replied Mrs Thonnings. "I don't fear the competition, there's only one way these new-fangled shops can look so fancy and that's by having over-priced stock."

"Have you been in to have a look?" asked Churchill.

"I most certainly have not! Why the very thought!"

"Didn't you say that you were sanguine and laissez faire about the whole thing?"

"Yes I am, although not quite enough to set foot in that place. I refuse to let it bother me, however."

"Good for you, Mrs Thonnings, that's the spirit. Well don't let us keep you, you need to get back to your own shop."

"Why?"

"You'll have presumably closed it while you went on your errand just now. There'll be customers waiting."

"Oh not at this time, it's usually quiet."

"But how do you know? You could be missing out on sales, Mrs Thonnings."

"I know that if my regular customers see the shop is shut, they'll merely return again later in the day."

"But they might not."

"They might go to Boutons et Rubans instead," added Pemberley.

"That over-priced establishment?" Mrs Thonnings gave a snort. "I think not." She paused and gave Mrs Churchill a sidelong glance. "You think I should be worried, don't you?"

"No, not at all."

"You think that I shouldn't be out on errands and should be in my shop all day to make sure none of my customers go off to Mrs Fancy-Pants."

"No, Mrs Thonnings, your errands are clearly important."

"Well they are indeed." She gave a wink.

"What do you mean by that?"

"What?"

"The wink."

"Oh." She gave Mrs Churchill a bashful look. "Just a little errand to meet my new man friend."

"Oh goodness, Mrs Thonnings. Can't it wait until you close the shop for the day?"

"No it can't, he has other commitments then. Well I must get back to the shop. Cheerio!"

"Good grief," commented Churchill as Mrs Thonnings went on her way. "Where does she find her man friends, Pembers?"

"She searches for them under rocks."

"That's rather unkind."

"Not necessarily, I think you'll find it's quite justified when you see some of her man friends."

"I have no interest in them. But what I do know is that she needs to be sprucing up her shop now that she has competition. All this gallivanting about is making her complacent and lackadaisical when it comes to her business. I fear this won't end well, Pembers."

Chapter 3

"It's SAD BUT, then again, he was as old as the hills," said Mr Simpkin the baker as he passed a bag of currant buns to Mrs Harris the following day.

"Didn't quite make it to one hundred," replied Mrs Harris. "Mind you, an age like that isn't natural. It goes against the grain. Threescore and ten is what it's supposed to be."

Churchill caught this snatch of conversation as she stepped into the bakery. "Apologies for the interruption," she said, "but who didn't make it to one hundred?"

"Dead, Pembers." Churchill arranged the chocolate eclairs on a plate on her desk as Oswald watched on, salivating. "The old Earl of Middlemop dead at the age of ninety-nine. Poor Tryphena must be terribly upset."

"She must be, but it can't have been an enormous shock."

"No, I suppose no one expects their ninety-nine year old father to go on forever. But it's upsetting all the same.

The end of an era. The lowering of a curtain. The dimming of the house lights."

Pemberley gave a sniff. "When you put it like that, it does sound so terribly final."

"It *is* final, there's no doubt about it. But I'm sure he led a long and wonderful life. He was an Earl! Not everybody gets to be an Earl, very few people do in actual fact. I'm quite sure he made the most of it with grand parties and shooting weekends and tea at royal residences and that sort of thing. Not a bad life really, is it? I'm quite sure that Tryphena and the rest of the Ridley-Balls family will commemorate his passing in a celebratory rather than mournful mood. To have been a member of the aristocracy for ninety-nine years! Life really doesn't get much better."

"I can't say that it appeals to me."

"You wouldn't want to be a member of the aristocracy, Pembers?"

"Oh no. They have too many rules about how things should be done. And I would have been married off and I certainly wouldn't have enjoyed that."

"How do you know you wouldn't have enjoyed it?"

"I just know. I much preferred my career as a companion to a lady of international travel."

"I see."

"The places I saw." A smile spread across Pemberley's face. "The things I did!"

"Yes you've told me all about those things plenty of times, there's no need to get bogged down with reminiscing again. Chocolate eclair?"

Pemberley gave a nod and Churchill brought the plate over to her desk. As she did so, she heard footsteps on the stairs which led up to their office. A moment later, Mrs

Thonnings stumbled into the room; her face was pale and she grasped a newspaper in one hand.

"Oh goodness, are you all right Mrs Thonnings?" Churchill steered her to the chair by her desk and sat her down.

"No, I'm not," she whimpered. Oswald greeted her, his tail wagging. Mrs Thonnings patted his head absent-mindedly and gave a sob.

Churchill took the newspaper from her hand and saw the headline announcing the Earl of Middlemop's death.

"It's awfully sad isn't it, Mrs Thonnings? Did you know him well?"

"Who?"

"The Earl of Middlemop." Churchill pointed to the picture of him on the front page of the *Compton Poppleford Gazette*. He was thin-faced with a sour expression and large ears.

"I knew him reasonably well."

"Oh dear, I am sorry. You do seem so terribly upset about it. He wasn't one of your, er... man friends was he?"

"What?" Mrs Thonnings stared at her incredulously.

"I didn't mean to offend, I do apologise. I just thought that, seeing as you're so upset about his death, that you might have known him well."

"Reasonably well but certainly not one of my *man friends*, what do you take me for, Mrs Churchill?"

"I'm sorry, perhaps I spoke out of turn. Miss Pemberley, perhaps you could make Mrs Thonnings a nice cup of tea?"

"Of course. And would you like the last eclair, Mrs Thonnings?" Pemberley brought the plate over to her.

"I don't think there's any need to stretch quite that far," interjected Churchill, but Mrs Thonnings' face had already brightened at the sight of the plate.

"Oh thank you, Miss Pemberley! Don't mind if I do."
She took the eclair and bit into it.

"The power of a sweet comestible, eh Mrs Thonnings?" commented Churchill enviously. "Quite a comfort in one's grief."

"What grief?" replied Mrs Thonnings through a mouthful.

"The Earl of course!"

"I have no idea why you think I held any affection for the Earl of Middlemop. He was a crusty old curmudgeon."

"Was he really?"

"Yes. Lived in that enormous house as big as a palace and spent most of his time in a little box room."

"Golly, Tryphena didn't tell me that."

"Well she wouldn't, she's his daughter."

"I see. Well why are you so upset about his passing?"

"I'm not! I couldn't care less!"

"So why on earth did you sink into that chair like a dying swan and eat the last eclair?"

"I came here to show you *that*." Mrs Thonnings pointed to the *Compton Poppleford Gazette* which Churchill had placed on her desk. "Turn to page four."

Saggy Elastic Leaves Locals Red-Faced
By Smithy Miggins

A local haberdashery shop has been accused of selling poor quality products after a stretch of wardrobe embarrassments. Readers have contacted this newspaper with reports that sub-standard elastic sold by 'Thonnings's Haberdashery' has led to drooping drawers and slumping socks.

All readers requested to remain anonymous, however the Compton Poppleford Gazette can exclusively report that:

A gentleman wearing sock suspenders, made with elastic from Thonnings's Haberdashery, discovered that his socks had gathered into ugly rolls at his ankles during a prestigious golf club dinner.

A lady's undergarments, recently repaired with elastic from Thonnings's Haberdashery, loosened during a shopping trip and came perilously close to slipping down altogether.

But in the most shocking incident of all, a lady has informed this newspaper that she had proudly worn a skirt she had made to a recent garden party. Her mistake? Using elastic for the waistband which she had bought from Thonnings's Haberdashery.

"I was just helping myself to another round of ham and tongue sandwiches when I heard an odd pinging sound," she writes in her letter. "Just as I began to wonder where the ping had come from, I felt a shameful slithering sensation as my skirt sank to my ankles. All of a sudden, my petticoat was on display for all to see. A wave of embarrassment washed over me as I attempted to haul my skirt up to my waist again. A kind lady supplied me with a safety pin but I was unable to eat anything else that afternoon and had to leave the party early."

What should have been an enjoyable afternoon for this poor lady had been thoroughly ruined by weak elastic. "I could ask Mrs Thonnings for a refund," she writes, "but nothing will ever compensate for the humiliation of the vicar laying eyes on my petticoat. I shall never live it down."

Our reporter tried to speak to Mrs Thonnings about these readers' claims, but her shop was closed with a sign on the door which said, 'back in fifteen minutes'.

Commenting on this spate of wardrobe embarrassments, the Mayor said, "I'm most concerned to hear that standards have slipped at one of the village's most valued shops. After a scandal like this, the proprietor needs to snap into action to pull back her customers. Sagging sales will squeeze her profits and, if she's not careful, it will be more than just the elastic which is over-stretched. I remain hopeful, however, that Thonnings's Haberdashery will bounce back."

"Oh goodness, Mrs Thonnings," said Churchill. "What dreadful news. Who are these anonymous people? Did they complain to you directly at all?"

"No, not a peep from any of them! I sell yards and yards of elastic every week. I've never had any complaints. If the lady whose skirt fell down at the garden party had brought it into the shop, I could have had a look at it for her. It's possible that there was a fault in its construction."

"Notice that she states that she had 'another round' of ham and tongue sandwiches," said Churchill. "She was putting too much strain on her waistband if you ask me. I should think any length of elastic is going to give way after an excessive consumption of ham and tongue sandwiches."

"The brand of elastic I sell is the best I know and it should be able to withstand extra strain without too much of a problem. I've used the same supplier for years! I've never known anything like this to happen before."

"Well I think it's the fault of the manufacturer," said Pemberley. "They must have changed their recipe."

"Perhaps they did, Miss Pemberley," replied Churchill. "But the sad fact of the matter is that the fault is being laid at Mrs Thonnings' door. I still think it rather odd that these customers didn't inform her of their wrinkled socks and unreliable undergarments and, instead, spoke to the *Compton Poppleford Gazette*. It wouldn't be my first course of action if my skirt fell down."

"I wish Smithy Miggins had spoken to me before this was published," said Mrs Thonnings. "Instead, the first I learnt about it was when I read the newspaper this morning."

"Well it seems that he tried but you were out."

"He could have returned fifteen minutes later!"

"Not if he had a strict deadline," said Pemberley. "Newspaper editors can be terribly bossy about deadlines and Smithy Miggins may not have had the time to return."

"Fifteen minutes is nothing at all!" protested Mrs Thonnings. "A proper news reporter would have given me the opportunity to speak. I would have been able to reassure customers that these were isolated incidents."

"Well that's the *Compton Poppleford Gazette* for you," said Churchill. "They like to print a scandalous story with only half the facts. If they had all the facts then it wouldn't be half as entertaining to read."

"So halving the facts doubles the entertainment," commented Pemberley.

"Exactly."

"It's not entertainment!" wailed Mrs Thonnings. "It's my livelihood!"

Churchill agreed with a sad shake of her head. "I know. These newspapers can be ruthless. They don't care who they upset, they just want the story."

Chapter 4

"I SHALL PAY dear Tryphena a visit after elevenses and pass on my condolences," said Churchill as she cut a slice of lemon cake the following morning. "She tells me that she lives in a delightful farmhouse on the Gripedown Estate. I'll take a little posy of flowers to cheer her up."

"Which means you'll have to take your chances with Mrs Crackleby the florist," said Pemberley.

"Oh dear, I'd forgotten what hard work she is. I can't say I'm in the mood for her this morning, is there another florist I can go to?"

"No, Mrs Crackleby saw to that."

"How?"

"I don't know exactly, but I do know that she served a prison sentence for it."

"Really?"

"It was a long time ago."

"And is she a reformed character?"

"I don't know, you'll have to be the judge of that yourself."

"On second thoughts, why don't I take Oswald to Tryphena's with me?" She glanced at the little dog lying in the middle of the floor. "He's such a lively, jolly fellow. No one can fail to be charmed by him."

"Not everyone takes to him, Mrs Churchill."

"Oh Tryphena will, she loves doggies."

"He can't go, he's asleep at the moment."

"No he's not, he's got his eyes open."

"That's how he sleeps."

"With his eyes open?"

"It's what his ancestors had to do in the wild to keep a watchful eye out for attackers."

"But he doesn't need to do that, he's nice and safe here in our office."

"It's in his instincts to do so. He wants to protect us."

"How adorable."

"He doesn't do it to be adorable, Mrs Churchill, he considers it his duty."

"Even more adorable. I don't think he's asleep, he's just lying there. Look, if I wave he'll glance over at me. See?"

"That's just his senses responding to a potential threat, he's not actually awake and looking at you, Mrs Churchill. However, if he decides you pose a danger of any sort then he'll awaken and alert the pack leader."

"Who's that?"

"Me."

"You? Why not me?"

"Because I'm the one who feeds him and gives him shelter."

"But it's my detective agency."

"He doesn't know that, does he? He considers me to be the leader of the pack."

"So what does he consider me to be, then?"

"I don't know. His litter mate perhaps."

"His litter mate? How could he possibly think that? I don't even look like his litter mate."

"He doesn't relate to you according to your appearance, it's all about the pack status."

"I don't understand all this pack business. You and I aren't Flemish lake dogs or whatever he is."

"Spanish water dog."

"That's the one. With a touch of terrier isn't it?"

"And a splash of spaniel."

"Right. Well I think it's a terrible shame he doesn't want to visit Tryphena with me. It looks like I shall have to take some flowers and endure Mrs Crackleby after all. I shall go now because she'll sell me three or four bunches in total and I'll have to bring some of them back here."

"You could always refuse to buy them."

"I've tried that before. But the woman has a certain way about her, doesn't she? It's probably how she managed to drive all the other florists out of Compton Poppleford. Mrs Thonnings could probably learn a thing or two from her when it comes to running a business."

"It's one thing running a business and quite another to conduct illegal activity."

"Golly, well the mind boggles. I'll just stay on the right side of her, that's probably best." Churchill got up from her chair and picked up her handbag. "Wish me luck then, Pembers."

She was just about to step through the door when she heard footsteps beyond it.

"Oh no, now there's a hindrance. There's always a hindrance when you're just about to do something, isn't there Pembers?"

She stepped back from the door as a stocky, wide-faced

lady in tweed and pearls bustled in. Steel waves of hair were tucked behind her large ears.

"Tryph!" exclaimed Churchill. "I was just about to—"

Tryphena's face crumpled. "Oh Annabel, it's dreadful I tell you. Dreadful! Poor old Daddy!"

"Oh goodness, yes, I'm so sorry." Churchill steered her friend over to the same chair she had sat Mrs Thonnings in the previous day. "I was just about to come and visit to pay my condolences."

"Oh thank you, Annabel." Tryphena pulled a handkerchief from her handbag and blew her nose loudly into it. "He didn't deserve such a thing!" she continued. "He was so looking forward to turning one hundred years old and now his future's been snatched away from him!"

"It is cruel indeed. He did very well to get to ninety-nine."

"He wanted to be the oldest man in Dorset!"

"Well he was certainly the richest."

"The richest in Wessex, not just Dorset."

"So I recall you saying, Tryphena."

"Who's the oldest man in Dorset, just out of interest?" asked Pemberley.

"Mr Ralph Boggert in Chipminster Wallis," sobbed Tryphena. "He's one hundred now. An age that my poor Daddy will never get to!"

"Miss Pemberley, please will you make us some tea?" asked Churchill. "She pulled a chair up next to her friend and patted her hand. "Well your father did very well indeed. I'm sure he had a long and happy life."

"He didn't!"

"But it was long."

"Not long enough!"

"My dear old Tryph, very few people ever reach the

age of ninety-nine. Could you really have expected your dear father to have lived many years longer?"

"Yes!"

"Really?"

"Yes, Annabel. I haven't told you yet have I? Daddy didn't merely die of old age. Someone murdered him!"

Chapter 5

"Someone murdered your father?" queried Churchill, thoroughly taken aback by the news. "And how?"

"He was poisoned!"

"Good grief. How horrific! How thoroughly awful! Why would someone do such a thing to a defenceless old man?"

"My sentiments exactly, Annabel. I just… well I'm just lost for words."

Pemberley brought in a tea tray and placed it on Mrs Churchill's desk.

"Would you like a slice of lemon cake, Tryphena?" asked Churchill.

"No thank you, I don't have any appetite at the moment."

"Understandable. The poor old Earl of Middlemop was poisoned, Miss Pemberley."

"Really? Why?"

"Well that's the question indeed. Have you any idea who would want to do this to your father, Tryphena?"

"None at all."

"Anyone he'd had a recent disagreement with? Or a long-standing feud perhaps?"

"No one I can think of at all."

"How did anyone realise he'd been poisoned?" asked Pemberley. "Given his age, it would have been easy to assume he'd died just because he was old."

"It was the doctor who suggested it," replied Tryhena. "We'd called him of course and when he examined poor Daddy he told us that he could smell almonds."

"Cyanide," said Churchill. "There's no doubt about it."

"That's right," said Tryphena. "So they took him away and this morning... well I don't like to think about it, but a post-mortem was carried out."

"And that confirmed what the doctor suspected, I take it?"

"Yes. It was cyanide." Tryphena gave a sob and blew her nose again.

"How was the poison administered?" asked Pemberley. "Was it in his food?"

"No, we think it had been put in his medicine."

"Good grief," said Churchill. "So terribly premeditated."

"I wondered at first if he'd simply taken too much of his medicine and that was why it had poisoned him," said Tryphena. "But the medicine wouldn't have ordinarily contained cyanide, would it?"

"It's not a common ingredient in medicine," said Churchill. "I take it the medicine has been examined and confirmed to be the source of the poisoning?"

"Inspector Mappin has given it to a chemist in Dorchester for analysis," replied Tryphena. "However the doctor is quite certain that the medicine was the source of the poison because it was the last thing Daddy consumed before retiring for the evening and its effects are apparently quite swift. Oh, how he must have suffered!"

"Your poor father. The medicine was something he took a regular dose of?"

"Yes, every evening."

"What sort of medicine is it?"

"Crumpot's Remedy Syrup. Daddy was prone to biliousness you see."

"Poor chap."

"He suffered from costive bowels."

"Oh dear."

"And terrible swelling after meals."

"How unpleasant," said Pemberley.

"It was. Sometimes nature's drainage can become quite clogged, can't it?"

"I believe so," replied Churchill.

"And Dr Crumpot's Remedy Syrup cleanses the organs of digestion by removing waste and foreign matter," added Tryphena.

"Foreign matter? Good grief."

"I know, it was all quite difficult for him. But he swore by his evening dose of Dr Crumpot's, he claimed that it changed the ferments of his digestive system."

"I think my own ferments are feeling rather affected now." Churchill was beginning to feel a little nauseous.

"Oh I am sorry. It really is such a terrible business."

"A terrible business indeed."

"I'm wondering, Annabel, if you'd perhaps like to help?"

"With what exactly?"

"With finding out who poisoned Daddy."

"Well I'd be delighted to do all I can, Tryphena!"

"Inspector Mappin is very good but when I suggested

we call in a detective from Scotland Yard, he wasn't happy about the suggestion at all."

"That doesn't surprise me."

"I really want everything possible done to find out who the murderer is."

"Tryphena, it would be a pleasure to find the culprit. Well, perhaps not a pleasure as such because, after all, there is no pleasure in the fact that someone murdered your father, but what I mean is—"

"We can all feel pleasure when the culprit is caught."

"Absolutely. That's what I meant."

"Wonderful." Tryphena tucked her handkerchief into her handbag and got to her feet. "Well thank you, Annabel, I'm most grateful. Perhaps you can meet me at Gripedown tomorrow morning. Shall we say ten o'clock?"

"Ten o'clock sharp it is."

"Poor old Tryph," said Churchill once her friend had departed. "How terribly unfortunate for her. Why on earth would anyone wish to murder her elderly father?" She helped herself to another slice of lemon cake.

"He was so old that it wouldn't have been long before he died anyway."

"Exactly! So for some reason someone wished to hasten his end."

"Who was set to benefit from his death?"

"You took the words right out of my mouth, Pembers. It is the first question which every self-respecting detective must ask himself."

"Or herself."

"That goes without saying, I was using himself as a generic term."

"Why not use herself as a generic term?"

"Well that's a valid question, Pembers, but we don't wish to distract ourselves with such debate at this moment. Now, when an extremely rich person is murdered there is one consideration which must be considered first and foremost, before anything else is even touched upon."

"What to bury them in."

"Not a consideration for a detective."

"But a consideration all the same. Some rich people have so many clothes they rarely wear the same thing twice. How does one even begin to decide on their burial suit? It will be quite easy when it's my time, Mrs Churchill, I only have one favourite cardigan."

"You'll need more than just a cardigan, Pembers."

"I'm not fussy which dress you choose, but the lilac cardigan is my favourite."

"Why should *I* be choosing which dress you're buried in Pembers? You're assuming that you're going to go before me."

"Oh I will, I'm sure of it."

"And it should be your next of kin which decides these things, not me!"

"Well that would be my nephew but he's hopeless at choosing outfits. Would you mind doing it?"

"Pembers, I do not wish to sit here discussing your burial outfit. It's morbid and we have urgent matters to attend to. We've been tasked with finding out who murdered the Earl of Middlemop. This isn't even a case we're meddling in, we've been specifically asked by his daughter. Now there's responsibility indeed. So let's focus on the matter at hand. Oh darn it, I can't even remember what we were discussing."

"The first and foremost consideration."

"Ah yes, that's right. In the case of a rich person it's the will, Pembers. Their will. That is the first and foremost consideration. Who is named in the Earl of Middlemop's will?"

"I don't know."

"Neither do I. Not yet anyway. So that's what we need to find out. Now here's the thing, Pembers, when murder is committed in respect of a will it's usually because the testator has expressed a wish in changing the said will. So, for example, there may have been a threat to have someone written out of it and the person who is about to be written out of it murders the testator before they have the opportunity to do it. Does that make sense? I think I've almost confused myself, there."

"I like the word testator, it's terribly legal and important sounding."

"It is, isn't it? In this case, our Earl of Middlemop is the testator."

"And he could have threatened to write Tryphena out of his will and she could have therefore murdered him before he found the chance to write her out."

"Exactly. Although Tryphena would never do such a thing."

"How do you know?"

"Because she's Tryph!"

"The Earl may not have threatened to write her out of his will, he may have merely mentioned to his lawyer that he wished to do so."

"Yes, and word could have somehow got back to Tryphena that it was her father's intention and then... actually not Tryphena, we're speaking hypothetically of course."

"Yes. It could be her or it could be someone else."

"Indeed. Likely to be someone else. Someone who was about to be disinherited and took umbrage at it."

"So the Earl of Middlemop's lawyer should be able to tell us who he was about to write out of his will."

"Indeed, it could be that simple. I have a hunch that it won't be though."

"Why not?"

"Because Tryphena would be able to find it out for herself quite easily."

"Unless she's the murderer."

"Which she can't possibly be."

"What's Oswald eating?"

"I don't know, is he eating something?"

"He's sitting next to your desk licking his lips."

"He's always licking his lips."

"He only does it when he's just eaten something."

"Possibly a crumb fell off my plate. Now where were we? Ah, yes the murder of a ninety-nine year old man. It's rather mysterious."

"I've come across mysteriouser."

"Well I suppose you would have, Pembers. One of Atkins's cases by any chance?"

"Yes it was actually. He once received an envelope filled with money from a mysterious Dr Htaed."

"Htaed? What's that? Dutch?"

"No, it's not. The money was payment for Atkins to investigate a murder. A wealthy lady had been found dead in her bedchamber and Atkins solved it, of course, but he never found out who hired him. He later realised that Htaed was death backwards." Pemberley followed this with a visible shudder.

"Of course it is! Anyone could have spotted that from the off."

"You thought it was Dutch, Mrs Churchill."

"That was my initial response, yes, but a moment later I realised it was death backwards. Quite an amateur attempt at being mysterious, don't you think? Htaed indeed. It's not even straightforward to pronounce. He could have at least plumped for something which rolls off the tongue such as... Dr Rillek for example."

"Rillek?"

"Yes."

"What's that?"

"Oh Pembers, do I have to spell it out? Killer of course. Dr Killer."

"That would be Rellik."

"Well it sounds very similar."

"But written down, it's quite different. It would confuse matters even more if it was translated as Dr Kellir."

"Let's focus instead on the matter at hand. I'm looking forward to our visit to Gripedown Hall tomorrow."

"So am I, we'll be able to have a good nosey around."

"Oh Pembers, that's not our reason for visiting! We have been tasked with finding a murderer, now let's get on with putting our incident board together."

Chapter 6

MR SPEAKMAN's taxi was just pulling away on Compton Poppleford high street the following day when it was flagged down by a lady with bright red hair.

"Oh golly, what does Mrs Thonnings want?" sighed Churchill as she sat on the back seat of the taxi with Pemberley and Oswald.

The driver braked sharply and uttered a string of curse words.

"There's no need for that Mr Speakman," scolded Churchill. "It's only Mrs Thonnings."

"She nearly killed 'erself!"

"What is it?" asked Churchill as she pulled the window down.

"I've worked it all out!" replied the haberdasher, excitedly thrusting her head into the rear of the car. "Where are you all off to?"

"Gripedown Hall."

"The Earl was poisoned wasn't he? That's what they're all saying. Why poison a man who was about to die anyway?"

"That's a discussion for another time, Mrs Thonnings. Why did you risk life and limb just now leaping in front of the car like that? What have you worked out?"

"Well I shall lose customers because of that awful newspaper story, won't I?"

"Hopefully not."

"Ah, but I will. The shop is already noticeably quieter."

"I'm sorry to hear it."

"And I'll tell you what's probably happening, my customers will now be going over to Mrs Fancy-Pants in her new shop."

"Well if it's true, then it's a terrible shame."

"It is true, I'm telling you! Who benefits from the news article, Mrs Churchill? Why, it's Mrs Fancy-Pants. She's behind this!"

"What do you mean?"

"She wrote all those letters to the newspaper! That's why no one complained to me directly. Those customers don't exist!"

"The droopy drawers and the slipping socks? They're a work of fiction?"

"Yes!"

"Yer do realise the meter's on?" called out Mr Speakman over his shoulder.

"Are you really saying that Mrs Bouton has written letters to the *Compton Poppleford Gazette* from fictional customers with fictional stories about failed elastic?"

"Yes, that's exactly what I'm saying!"

"Do you have any proof?"

"No, that's what I need you to help me with, Mrs Churchill. I need proof that she's behind this. Will you help me?"

"Of course, although the idea does seem a little far-fetched. Are you sure you're not mistaken, Mrs Thonnings?"

"Quite sure. Thank you for helping. I think I've been quite clever to work this out, is there a vacancy yet for me at Churchill's Detective Agency?"

"Not quite yet, Mrs Thonnings. We must go, the meter's ticking and it's probably added a shilling already knowing the fares that Mr Speakman charges."

"Yer do realise I'm sat just in front of you, don't yer?" responded the driver.

"Indeed. Now we must away. Cheerio Mrs Thonnings!" Churchill gave a royal wave and they were off.

After a short journey, the taxi arrived at the tall iron gates of Gripedown Hall.

"S'pose you'll want me to drive you up to the 'ouse," grumbled Mr Speakman.

"How long is the driveway?"

"Long."

"Then yes please, take us up to the house."

He begrudgingly got out of the car to open the gates before returning and driving them through. Ahead of them, a long driveway wound through a wide expanse of green.

"This will be the deer park," observed Churchill. "How nice to have one's own park of deer."

"Ready supply o' venison, that's for sure," said Mr Speakman. "Big old place, all right. S'pose the whole lot will go to the grandson."

"He's the next in line?"

"Yeah, the son popped 'is clogs about ten year ago."

"So the Earl's grandson has become the heir," said Churchill. "Who is he?"

"Humphrey Ridley-Balls. He'll be the ninth Earl o' Middlemop now. Although there's a bit o' funny business about 'im."

"Funny business? In what way?"

"Long story, most of it proberly ain't true anyways. Look there's the 'ouse."

A large grey stone building now loomed into view. It had a steeply pitched roof, tall chimneys and countless little windows.

"I had expected something a little prettier," commented Churchill. "In a warm hue of Dorset sandstone, perhaps, and a grand entrance with columns."

"I'd say it was grand enough," responded Mr Speakman. "Dunno they're born half these people. Old Middlemop lived in a big place like this and never 'ad a nice word ter say ter no one."

"Maybe that's why he was murdered," said Pemberley.

"No one deserves to be murdered, Miss Pemberley. Not even grumpy earls."

The taxi pulled up next to a fountain with three tiers of cherubs and lions. The two ladies paid their fare and climbed out. As they walked up to the house, Tryphena appeared on the front steps and greeted them.

"Thank you so much for coming, both of you."

"Inspector Mappin's not here is he?"

"No the police left about an hour ago."

"Good, I can't imagine him taking kindly to our involvement. Have you told Mappin that you've asked us to help with the investigation?"

"Not yet."

"Oh well, all in good time, Tryph, you have a lot to think about. This is quite some place here." Churchill peered up at a stone eagle which screeched silently down at them from above the doorway. "How long has it been in your family?"

"About three hundred years. The first earl was gifted the house by the king in return for victory at some battle of something or other."

"How lovely."

"Come on in ladies!" The two ladies and their dog followed Tryphena up the steps and through the large doors which were propped open with two brass lions. Churchill's mouth hung open as she surveyed the grand hallway with its large chandelier and sweeping staircase at the end. To the far right of the hallway, a maid knelt on the floor and polished the tiles with a cloth.

Tryphena gestured at the portraits on the wall. "The requisite ancestors, of course."

"Naturally."

"You can tell they're all related," commented Pemberley. "Just look at those ears."

"You grew up in this place, Tryphena?" Churchill swiftly asked.

"I did indeed. I have fond memories of it too. As children we used to roller-skate along the corridors, there was trouble if Nanny caught us in the act, mind you! And there were games of hide and seek which took hours and hours because there were so many places to hide. My brother Horace once went undiscovered in a room in the east wing for two days."

"Gosh, why didn't he come out before then?"

"Well he was rather frozen in fear. He was too terrified."

"By what?"

"The grey lady."

"A ghost?"

"Ghost?" repeated Pemberley, tremulously.

"Yes, we have three of them here. There's the boy in the attic, the horseman on the driveway and the grey lady in the east wing."

Churchill gave a shiver while attempting to shrug off such supernatural nonsense.

"The boy in the attic was beaten to death for blotting his copybook," continued Tryphena.

"Oh, how awful!" cried Pemberley.

"He had a rather strict governess," continued Tryphena.

"An understatement by the sounds of things."

"He was the seventh son of the third earl or something or other. Most sad. The headless horseman is the ghost of a messenger who was the bearer of bad news. It's said that the second earl was so enraged by the message that he lopped the man's head off with a sword and legend has it that the horseman gallops along the driveway whenever the Ridley-Balls family is about to receive bad news."

"I'd certainly consider it a bad omen if I saw a headless horseman galloping down my driveway," said Pemberley with a shiver.

"You don't have a driveway, Miss Pemberley."

"Thank goodness. In fact I'm rather relieved that my abode is humble, the bigger the house the more chance there is of a ghost living in it."

"Or three. And what of the grey lady, Tryphena?"

"I think she's meant to be the wife of the fifth earl or someone or other. He was killed in battle somewhere and she never accepted it, in grief she wandered the corridors and staircases until she collapsed from hunger and exhaustion and died on the spot. It's said that a sighting of her is a portent of someone's death."

"Crikey."

"All nonsense of course!" laughed Tryphena.

"Of course!" Churchill gave a relieved chuckle. "You haven't seen any of these spooks I take it?"

"Of course not."

"But what of poor Horace hiding in fear in the east wing for two days?" asked Pemberley.

"Oh I think he made up the sighting of the grey lady just to scare us. And I don't think he was really there for two days, I think it was about two hours."

"Phew!"

"Other people have seen the ghosts though."

"Really?"

"Oh yes, the servants seem to see them on a regular basis. They're a superstitious lot though, aren't they? I think they make these stories up to entertain each other half the time. Now let me show you Daddy's rooms." She walked off towards the large staircase.

"We must get our notebooks out, Pembers," whispered Churchill as she rummaged about in her handbag. "It's important to show that we're taking all this extremely seriously. We've been tasked with an important job."

"I didn't bring my notebook."

"Why ever not?"

"I didn't think I'd need it."

"Of course you need a notebook!" Churchill pulled hers out of her handbag. "Here, have mine and here's a pen too. Write everything down."

"Everything?"

"Everything that you consider relevant, Pembers. You've been in this line of work for a while now, surely you know what needs writing down and what doesn't?"

"Yes, and I don't usually write anything down. I just store it in my head."

"Writing it down makes us appear professional."

"So that's why you want me to do it? To appear professional rather than serve any useful purpose?"

"Since you put it that way, then yes. Come on, let's catch up with Tryph."

Chapter 7

"Do LET me know if you need a hand up the stairs," called Tryphena from the top of the staircase.

"A hand? What do you take me for, Tryph?"

"Well they're not always easy to navigate when you're getting long in the tooth."

Churchill laughed this off and began skipping up the stairs as quickly as she could.

A few moments later, she leant against the banister at the top, light-headed with exertion. "So H-H-Humphrey Ridley-Balls inherits th-th-this place?"

"Would you like to sit down and rest for a while, Annabel?"

"N-n-no, I'm quite fine thank you."

"There was no need to quite rush like that."

"I'm quite all right, thank you Tryphena. Now, about Humphrey—"

"We don't know about him yet," she snapped as she strolled off along a corridor.

Churchill discerned from this that Tryphena had little

fondness for her nephew. She shot Pemberley a wary glance and the two ladies followed after her.

"Is he the heir?" Churchill ventured.

"In theory."

"On our way here, the taxi driver said—"

"Here are Daddy's rooms," interrupted Tryphena, pushing open a large door. They stepped into a spacious oak-panelled room filled with sunlight from three tall windows which overlooked the driveway. Stiff-backed leather chairs were placed around a card table and an imposing marble fireplace dominated one end of the room. Above it, a thin, large-eared man scowled out of a painting. Wisps of white hair covered his head and chin and he sat slumped in a chair, his hand resting on the head of an attentive brown spaniel.

"Your father, Tryphena?" asked Churchill, her mind desperately searching for something complimentary to say about his appearance.

"That's right," came the proud reply.

"Very distinguished."

"Oh he was extremely distinguished."

"I like the dog," commented Pemberley.

"That's Margery," replied Tryphena. "You'll meet her soon enough, she's missing him terribly."

As Churchill glanced around the room she noticed that there were few personal effects, in fact it had the appearance of a room which hadn't been used much at all.

"I'll show you the rest of Daddy's rooms," said Tryphena, heading for a door beside the fireplace.

Churchill and Pemberley were shown several more drab oak-panelled rooms, each half-empty with just a few pieces of old furniture.

"Where was he found?" asked Churchill. "When he... well, you know, after he had died?"

"On his bed," replied Tryphena. "I'll show you."

Churchill gave a shudder. She didn't like the old-fashioned rooms and the smell of the musty closed-up air within them. She certainly didn't like the thought of the boy in the attic, the headless horseman and the grey lady in the east wing.

"Are we in the west wing?" she asked.

"No, the east."

"Oh."

They stepped into a room containing an enormous four poster bed hung with brocade curtains. Churchill felt sure that the gloom in this room was due to the fact the Earl had recently died here. The temperature felt lower and she sensed a chill in her bones. Pemberley didn't look particularly comfortable either and Oswald stood close to her legs, his eyes wide and his ears pricked.

"So this is the place," said Churchill quietly. "Where you found him?"

"Oh no, Daddy didn't use any of these rooms, he just walked through them to get to his bedroom."

"This wasn't his bedroom?"

"No, it's through here." She walked on to the next door. "He liked to sleep in the room which once served as his dressing room. The other rooms here are all very grand but he said they had terrible draughts. He much preferred his truckle bed."

"All this space just going to waste?" exclaimed Pemberley.

"It's not going to waste, it stores some delightful old masters."

"Who are they?"

"The pictures on the wall."

"Oh them."

They followed Tryphena through to a small room with

a narrow bed in one corner, an old writing desk and a little fireplace. In front of the fireplace sat a worn easy chair.

"This is where your father spent his time?" asked Churchill.

"That's right, he was very happy here."

Churchill considered the sheer size of the house as she surveyed the modest room they now stood in.

"And the bathroom is through this way," said Tryphena opening another door and showing them a little room tiled in green and white. "Daddy had this bathroom put in just a few years ago, it was where he conducted his ablutions."

"Naturally. And his bottle of remedy syrup was stored where?"

"On the shelf above the sink." Tryphena pointed to the shelf which now had only a cup with a toothbrush sitting in it. "The police took away his medicine bottle."

"And who had access to it?"

"Well all of the servants I suppose. Mr Charles Porge served as both butler and valet. Mrs Susannah Surpant is the housekeeper and then there is the maid who cleaned his rooms every day and brought him refreshments."

Churchill glanced around the little bathroom and then stepped back into the small room which contained the Earl's truckle bed.

"Apart from the servants, was there anyone else who regularly came to these rooms?" she asked.

"No one at all. No one else had any reason to."

"And, to access this bathroom, the murderer would have had to walk through all the rooms we have just walked through. How many are there?"

"Five."

"And there's no shortcut such as another staircase? A secret passage we should consider?"

"Nothing of the sort."

"The murderer must have felt quite confident that he or she wouldn't be seen. Either that or it was someone who was meant to be here such as one of the servants. We need a list of everyone who was seen in these rooms on that day."

"I can't give you a complete list, Annabel, but we could ask Mrs Surpant." Tryphena pulled a grimace. "I don't like the woman."

"What's wrong with her?"

"You'll soon see."

"Right, well what did your father do on his last day, Tryph?"

Churchill gave the notebook in Pemberley's hand a pointed glance and her assistant readied herself with her pencil.

"Well he didn't do a great deal," replied Tryphena. "On account of his age."

"Of course."

"He rose early and Gertie brought him his breakfast. Then Mr Porge ran his bath, he dressed and went for his daily constitutional around the rose garden."

"How nice."

"He had his lunch out on the terrace, it was a lovely warm day. After lunch he came back to his room for an afternoon nap and that was always at two o'clock. By three o'clock he was up and about again and I had a little chat with him that afternoon by the fountain."

"The one out the front with all the lions and cherubs on it?"

"Yes, that one."

"And what time was that?"

"About four o'clock. Then Daddy had tea in the library and returned to his room at six o'clock at which time Gertie the maid brought him his supper. Mr Porge was up there with him for a little while. When Gertie went to collect the supper tray at about eight o'clock, she discovered him... oh!" Tryphena clasped her handkerchief to her face.

"There, there, Tryph."

Churchill waited patiently for her friend to soothe herself before continuing, "and it's been ascertained that the poison was in your father's remedy syrup."

"Yes, and the lid had been left off it. He hadn't even had time to replace the lid before he began to feel the effects... oh, just terrible."

"And he staggered into his room and lay on his bed."

"Yes, we think he fell onto it."

"I see. And he took the remedy syrup every evening?"

"Yes, it was his habit to have two spoonfuls of it every night before retiring. It kept everything working as regular as clockwork, you see."

"So he took it the previous evening with no ill effects. However, the following evening, tragedy struck."

"Yes."

"Now then, Tryphena, who was set to benefit from your father's death?"

"Benefit?" Her face fell. "Benefit from his death? No one! We're all completely devastated by his death!"

"My apologies, Tryph, I used the wrong phrase. I meant the will, you see. Who was named in the will?"

"Oh here we go, it always comes down to money doesn't it?" Tryphena rubbed her hand across her brow. "Just because Daddy was the richest man in Wessex."

"I realise this isn't easy, but don't you think that his money could have been a motivation for the murderer?"

"Well it could have had something to do with it, I suppose. But you mustn't make assumptions, Annabel!"

"I won't make any assumptions, I'm merely exploring all the many possible different avenues of investigation."

"I see."

"So do you know who was named in his will?"

"No, not yet. Mr Verney has all the details and he's meeting with us all on Tuesday."

"I see."

"And I'm really not bothered at all about the contents of the will," continued Tryphena. "I merely want to find out who put poison in Daddy's remedy syrup!"

"Of course. However, let's begin the avenue of investigation concerning the will."

"Oh must we?"

"We could at least begin a little stroll along it and when we've had enough we can turn back and wander down another avenue."

"Oh all right."

"So who is likely to have been named in your father's will, Tryphena. Presumably his children?"

"Yes. So that would be me and Cairistiona."

"I see." Churchill wondered how Pemberley was going to spell this in her notebook. "Your brother or sister?"

"Sister!"

"Oh I do apologise, I should have known that from the name."

"She's been spending a little more time here in the past few months. I get the impression that all is not well at home." She lowered her voice for this latter point, as if she didn't want anyone else to hear it.

"I see. Any more siblings, Tryph?"

"Well my brother, Horace, is deceased."

"Oh I am sorry to hear that. If he were still alive then he would presumably have inherited this estate?"

"Well I'm not sure about that, Daddy didn't agree with primogeniture."

"Is she another sister?"

"No, Annabel!" Tryphena laughed. "Oh you are funny. The right of primogeniture is when the estate passes to the firstborn son."

"Oh of course, yes that. I knew that really. I always think it's rather unfair, don't you?"

"Yes. And so did Daddy so I'm quite sure it wouldn't have all gone to Horace anyway, if he were still alive that is."

"And Humphrey is his son?"

"Yes." Her face stiffened.

"So he is the assumed heir, however it's all dependent on the will I suppose. Does he have siblings?"

"Yes he has three older sisters, Delila, Belinda and Clarissa."

"And the least said about them, the better too?"

"No, they're alright actually."

"So your brother's four children could have been left something in your father's will?"

"They could have been, although Humphrey shouldn't receive anything."

"Why not?"

"It's a long story, Annabel. Oh look, here's Margery!"

The brown spaniel from the painting entered the room, her tail wagging. She and Oswald began sniffing each other curiously.

"Poor Margery," lamented Tryphena. "She's missing Daddy so much."

"It looks like Oswald is cheering her up," said Pemberley. The two dogs began to skip about, then both ran out of the room.

"You'll want to speak to the other members of the household," said Tryphena. "I'll introduce them to you now."

She led the way out of the bathroom.

Chapter 8

CHURCHILL AND PEMBERLEY followed Tryphena along a lengthy, dingy corridor. The wallpaper was faded and heavy curtains hung at the windows. Churchill paused to glance out of one and admired the view of the well-manicured grounds. In the middle of a lawn, she saw someone being pushed in a bath chair.

"A relative of yours, Tryphena?" she asked.

"Aunt Nora," she replied, once she'd peered out. "Daddy's sister. She's ninety-seven now and rarely leaves her rooms. She must be on her weekly outing in the gardens, that's her nurse, Nellie Hallwick, pushing her. The footmen have to carry both her and the bath chair down several flights of stairs, she's up on the top storey you see. It's a lot of work for everyone."

"I expect it is. Wouldn't it be easier for Aunt Nora to have rooms on the ground floor?"

"Well it would, but that was Daddy for you. He didn't like to change things about. That said, Aunt Nora was still able to get about on her own as recently as three months ago. Thank goodness Daddy never lost the use of his legs, he'd have been terribly miserable about it."

"Miss Pemberley and I will need to speak with your aunt during the course of our investigation."

"You can try. She's easily upset by impromptu visitors though. She'll need a few days' notice so I'll ask her nurse to telephone you."

"Golly, all right then."

The ladies continued on their way and Churchill startled when she saw a tall, black figure gliding towards them.

"Here's Mrs Surpant the housekeeper," said Tryphena.

"Thank goodness for that. I thought it was a…"

"Ghost?" She gave a laugh. "No, but I can understand why you would think that."

They stopped and watched the figure approach. The housekeeper's grey hair was scraped back from her gaunt face and her pale eyes stared at them.

"Mrs Surpant, may I introduce Mrs Churchill and Miss Pemberley of Churchill's Detective Agency," said Tryphena.

"It's a pleasure to meet you, Mrs Surpant," said Churchill.

"And may I ask what you're doing here?" replied the housekeeper.

Tryphena forced a laugh as if to mask the abruptness of the question. "I've asked Mrs Churchill and Miss Pemberley to investigate Daddy's death, Mrs Surpant."

Churchill felt the housekeeper's eyes sweep over her like a frosty breeze.

"Marvellous," replied Mrs Surpant with a thin smile. "May I ask why the police inspector is insufficient?"

"Oh he's not insufficient at all but I think we need all the help we can get. I'm sure that, like me, you're quite desperate to find out who caused such mischief to Daddy."

"It was more than a little mischief, Madam."

"Well it was, yes, it was terribly awful and I don't feel that I can, oh, excuse me. Silly me!" Tryphena pulled her handkerchief from her sleeve and dabbed at her eyes. "I really must have this solved," she continued once she had recovered a little. "I want to find the culprit and my dear friend Annabel here is so good at these things that I would be a fool not to enlist her help to be quite frank with you."

Churchill attempted a jolly chuckle which quickly evaporated within the gloomy corridor. "Mrs Surpant, please do accept my condolences on the death of your employer, the Earl of Middlemop. I never met the great man in person but my dear friend Tryphena has told me a good deal about him."

"Thank you, Mrs Churchill. I like to think I was of great assistance to him during his final years. In fact, I know I was because he told me so."

"That must have been nice to hear."

"Well he appreciated what I did for him. He liked my company. He didn't receive many visitors, you see."

"I visited every Sunday afternoon," piped up Tryphena.

"Yes, you did."

"And that wasn't enough for him?"

"Well the other six-and-a-half days would have been very empty if I hadn't been around to fill them."

"How very generous of you Mrs Surpant," retorted Tryphena. "That is, one might consider it so if you hadn't received a salary, board and lodging in return."

Churchill examined the clasp of her handbag while the two ladies glared at one another. After an uncomfortable silence, she ventured, "perhaps I can ask you a few questions, Mrs Surpant?"

"I'm afraid now would not be an appropriate time," came the reply. "Today is wash day."

"I'm quite sure that wash day can wait, Mrs Surpant," snapped Tryphena. "My poor dear old Daddy is dead! Now please do spare a moment to answer the questions of my good friend, Mrs Churchill."

The housekeeper's mouth puckered up so small that it almost disappeared into her face. Then she took a deep breath through her nose and her mouth reappeared. "I've already spoken to the Inspector," she said. "I don't have anything else to add."

"But I would like you to speak to Mrs Churchill too, she's a private detective. Please, Mrs Surpant, if not for my sake then at least for Daddy's sake. You adored him, I know you did. Don't you wish to catch the person who did this?"

The housekeeper's face softened a little and she checked the watch which was attached to her belt. "I've no doubt that the culprit will be caught soon enough. But I can find a little time now if that pleases you, Madam."

"Oh thank you!" enthused Tryphena. "Now do fire away, Annabel!"

Churchill cleared her throat. "Perhaps you can tell us what you remember from the Earl of Middlemop's last day, Mrs Surpant?"

"All of it?"

"Yes please."

"From the moment I rose at five o'clock that morning?"

"Yes please."

"Very well then. If wash day is now deemed of little importance, despite the fact that it's been an essential weekly fixture for the past forty years, then I shall tell you, Mrs Churchill." The housekeeper proceeded to list out everything she'd undertaken that morning to a degree of detail which Churchill regarded as unnecessary. The intended effect, she decided, was to force her to wish she'd never asked.

She grew more interested, however, as Mrs Surpant reached late afternoon.

"While the Earl of Middlemop was out with Miss Ridley-Balls by the fountain, Gertie the maid lit the fire in his room and discovered that the chimney was refusing to draw. We had to get the handyman in to unblock it."

"And who is the handyman?"

"Mr Vincent Goldbeam. He lives on the estate."

"So both Gertie and Mr Goldbeam were in the Earl's rooms while he was out by the fountain?"

"That's correct. And quite normal, too, I should add."

"When did you last visit the Earl's rooms that day?"

"I checked the room after the chimney blockage had been removed and all was well."

"May I ask what had been blocking the chimney?"

"An old bird's nest I think Mr Goldbeam said it was."

"So you were in the Earl's rooms as well that afternoon?"

"Of course. As I have just said. And then I went off to ensure the mirrors were being cleaned properly. The ones in the ballroom are particularly troublesome…"

Churchill endured another few minutes of Mrs Surpant's digression but was determined to show that her patience wasn't being worn down.

"And what time did the Earl return to his rooms?" She asked.

"At six o'clock. Gertie brought him his supper and the butler, Mr Porge, attended to his needs."

"Was it usual for the Earl to dine in his rooms in the evening?"

"Quite usual, yes. He said he no longer had the patience for sitting at a long table in the large dining room where he couldn't hear anyone speak properly and there was a terrible draught."

"And then he took a dose of Dr Crumpot's Remedy Syrup after his supper and it was this dose which was to kill him?"

"Indeed it was, sadly."

"So when was the last time you saw your employer?"

"When he was sitting in the library."

"This was after he was by the fountain?"

"Yes."

"And what was he doing in the library?"

"Muttering to himself angrily."

"About what?"

"I couldn't understand it all, but he appeared to be annoyed about the fountain."

"What could have possibly annoyed him about the fountain?"

"I have no idea, but I'm sure Miss Ridley-Balls will be able to tell you."

The housekeeper's eyes now rested on Tryphena.

"I see, thank you Mrs Surpant. So the last time you saw the Earl was in the library and he seemed angry to you?"

"Yes."

"Was that unusual?"

"Not completely, however he appeared to be a little more aeriated than usual."

"Did that concern you?"

"A little, but I decided that some tea might soothe him and that was being prepared at the time. In fact, I was with him when Gertie brought in the tea tray and set everything out on the table. It was the everyday teapot, the one with the slight chip in the spout which I would quite happily dispose of but the Earl was quite partial to—" Once again the housekeeper began describing irrelevant details.

"And the circumstances in which he was found?" interrupted Churchill, keen to get on with things.

"Found?"

"When he had died."

"Oh. Yes, Gertie found him." Her voice was low and sombre now. "She was terribly upset and raised quite a hue and cry dashing about the house in a state of hysteria. We all thought it was natural of course, that he had merely passed away due to some weakness or failure of something. He was ninety-nine years old so I don't think anyone laboured under the misapprehension that he had many years ahead of him. But to discover that it was poison..." The housekeeper now glared at Miss Ridley-Balls. "I don't understand how anybody could do such a thing."

Chapter 9

"How I detest Mrs Surpant," muttered Tryphena as they descended the wide staircase. "A thoroughly miserable woman, I don't know why Daddy employed her."

"Perhaps there's a fun side to her?" responded Churchill.

"Apparently there is, Daddy told me that she was wonderful company after a few sherries."

"After she'd had a few sherries or he had?"

"That's a good question." Tryphena paused halfway on the stairs to consider it further. "I had always assumed it was Daddy who'd consumed the sherry. I can't imagine Mrs Surpant partaking, can you?"

"No."

"Well there we go then." She resumed her descent. "Sherry is often the only way to endure difficult company."

"I couldn't agree more, although I'm also quite partic- ular to brandy and lovage. Difficult company is soon forgotten about after that."

"You'll want to speak to Mr Porge the butler," said Tryphena, once they were at the foot of the stairs.

"Is he better company than Mrs Surpant?"

"Only marginally."

"I see."

"He's out on an errand at the moment so you'll need to speak to him on your next visit. There's also Gertie the maid."

"Naturally. Are you writing this down, Miss Pemberley?"

Her assistant gave a nod.

"And we'll also need to speak to the handyman, Mr Goldbeam," said Churchill.

"Why?" queried Tryphena.

"Because he was in your father's rooms on the day your father was poisoned."

Tryphena gave a laugh. "Mr Goldbeam would hardly wish to poison Daddy!"

"We must speak to him all the same."

"Well I shall think he's going to be highly amused to be considered a suspect."

"He's not a suspect, merely a person of interest. He was in your father's rooms at a time when the poison could have been put in his remedy syrup. It's important that we speak with him. He lives on the estate, is that right?"

"Yes, he's in one of the cottages down at Sparrow's Bottom."

Churchill noticed Pemberley suppress a giggle.

"And where might that be?"

"Follow the track which runs west of the orangery, it's a fifteen minute walk or so." Tryphena glanced at the grand-father clock. "Goodness, I need to be on my way to the solicitor, Mr Verney. There are a lot of matters to settle."

"He's reading the contents of the will on Tuesday, is that right?"

"Yes. And you may attend if you wish."

"Thank you Tryphena. And, just quickly, your sister…"

"Cairistiona."

"Yes, her. Does she live locally?"

"About fifteen miles from here, at Hoffmanner Manor. She's married to Captain Vigors-Slipcote. You must meet her too, of course, she's a regular visitor so I'm sure it won't be long before you bump into one another. Right, I must be off! Thank you so much for your help, Annabel. And to you too, Miss Pemberley. Do come and go as you please here, I realise there's a lot to do."

She bid them farewell and strode off through one of the many doors leading from the hallway.

"Well there we have it, Pembers," said Churchill. "Did you get all that?" She glanced at the notebook in Pemberley's hand. "You don't appear to have written very much. What does that say? *Margery*?"

"I like Margery. Oswald's very fond of her."

"What about the rest of it? I told you to write it all down!"

"I had planned to but I was too busy listening."

"Oh good grief, Pembers! Now let's go and visit Mr Goldbeam at Sparrow's Bottom. I do hope he offers us some elevenses. I feel like I've gone quite without so far today."

The two ladies left the house and surveyed the ornate fountain in front of them.

"I wonder if this is the same fountain which Mrs Surpant mentioned," pondered Churchill. "She said the Earl was out by the fountain and afterwards he was angry in the library. She suggested that he was annoyed, for some reason, by the fountain."

"And do you remember that when you asked Mrs

Surpant what had annoyed him about the fountain, she said that Tryphena would be able to tell you."

"That's right!"

"But you forgot to ask Tryphena about it."

"Silly me, so I did."

"Did you notice that she didn't volunteer the information?"

"She didn't but then poor Tryph does have a lot on her mind at the moment."

"Did you notice she also managed to change the subject each time you attempted to discuss Humphrey Ridley-Balls? I don't think she's being straight with you, Mrs Churchill. A little odd really considering that you're best friends."

"Of course she's being straight with me, Pembers!"

"But surely you admit there are some questions she didn't answer?"

"Yes of course and that's because we're going to be speaking to her a great deal more over the coming days. We couldn't possibly overwhelm her with every question under the sun in one go. That would be unreasonable."

"You don't think she's taking advantage of your friendship to wriggle her way out of tricky questions?"

"Of course not!"

"Perhaps she thinks you'll go easy on her because you're her friend. Perhaps that's why she asked you to investigate in the first place?"

"It's nothing of the sort! Now that's enough, Pembers! We have a lot to be getting on with. Let's forget about the fountain and the Earl's inexplicable anger about it for the moment and head on down to Sparrow's Bottom to find Mr Goldbeam."

"Don't you think it's also odd that we have to wait for a telephone call before we can speak to Aunt Nora?"

"No, not odd at all. Aunt Nora is clearly one of those elderly ladies who's easily upset by things. Now come along."

Churchill began to stride away from the fountain, hoping that she was heading in the right direction.

"And Humphrey Ridley-Balls?" queried Pemberley as she jogged to catch up with her.

"There'll be a family secret or scandal about him, Pembers. There always is. These upper-class families have more skeletons in their closets than…"

"What?"

"I'm trying to think of someone else who would have a lot of skeletons in their closet."

"Mrs Thonnings?" suggested Pemberley.

"Do you think she has a lot of skeletons in her closet?"

"Yes, that's why I suggested her."

"Goodness, I wonder what?"

"I don't know. They're all in her closet."

Churchill gave a sigh. "Let's go and find Sparrow's Bottom and perhaps we'll find out what's happened to Oswald too."

Mr Goldbeam was a squat, square-faced man with a slack jaw and oil-stained overalls. He was wielding a spanner on a motorcycle as the two ladies approached the huddle of cottages nestled in the little valley of Sparrow's Bottom.

"What can I do yer for?" he asked, his eyes firmly fixed on the job at hand. Any hope that he'd invite them into his cottage for elevenses now seemed remote.

Churchill introduced herself and Pemberley and explained why they were visiting. Mr Goldbeam gave a grunt and wrenched something off his machine.

"Look at the state o' that spark plug," he stated,

holding it up for inspection. "No wonder she weren't firin' on all cylinders."

"I'm familiar with that feeling," said Churchill.

"Well don't go askin' me to check yer spark plugs." He pointed his spanner at her. "I wouldn't know where to look for 'em!" He gave a gravelly chuckle and Churchill responded with an uneasy laugh.

"You visited Gripedown Hall to unblock the Earl's chimney, is that correct?" she asked.

"Aye, that's correct. On the day 'e died."

"Can you recall what time it was?"

"Lemme see now…" He tapped the end of the spanner on his palm as he thought. "It would have been about four."

"Four o'clock?"

"Yeah that would be 'bout right."

"And how long were you there for?"

"About twenny minutes."

"And did you see the Earl during your visit?"

"No I didn't."

"Did you see anyone else in his rooms?"

"Only the 'ousekeeper. She showed me there and then I laid out me dust sheets and got on with it."

"The housekeeper left you to get on with it?"

"Yeah."

"Did she go into the bathroom while you were there?"

"Not that I know of. Couldn't tell you if truth be told, I had me 'ead stuck up a chimney."

"And may I ask what was blocking the chimney?"

"Old Ridley-Balls had shoved some papers up there."

"Do you know why?"

He gave a shrug. "No idea. P'rhaps he was tryin' to hide 'em."

"Hide them from who?"

"How would I know?"

"I'm not expecting you to, I just wondered if you had an inkling."

"No inklin'."

"Did you see what the papers were when you pulled them out?"

"Nah, never looked at 'em. I just put 'em on the table, twiddled me brush in the flue a bit more, then went on me way."

"Do you know what became of the papers?"

"No idea."

"Did you tell anyone what you'd found?"

"Oh yeah, I said to that ole housekeeper woman, I says 'the old boy's shoved some papers up there, I've pulled 'em out and left 'em on a table'."

"That's what you said to her."

"Absolutely it was."

"Then you went on your way."

"Then I went on me way."

"Did you not think it a little odd that the Earl of Middlemop put some papers up his chimney?"

"Didn't fink much of it. He was old weren't he? Not quite with it 'alf the time."

"I've noticed something rather odd about this case," said Churchill as they walked back towards the house.

"I've noticed several things rather odd about this case," replied Pemberley. "Which one in particular do you have in mind?"

"I'm sure Mrs Surpant told us that Mr Goldbeam pulled an old bird's nest out of the Earl's chimney. However, Mr Goldbeam seemed quite adamant just then that he pulled out a bundle of papers. One of them must be lying."

"Or merely mistaken."

"Possibly."

"I think it more likely that they're lying. Both of them could be lying and it could have been something else altogether. In fact, perhaps they're both lying that the chimney was blocked at all."

"Goodness, Pembers, you are in a sceptical mood today."

"I am yes. I don't like any of these people and I don't trust a single word they say."

"Oh look, here's our little dog here to cheer us up. Just in time!"

Oswald cantered across the lawn to them with his new friend Margery. The two ladies made a fuss of them both.

"And here comes someone else to cheer us up," announced Pemberley.

"Really?" Churchill looked up to see a brown-whiskered police inspector dismounting from his bicycle. "Oh. Inspector Mappin. You had me fooled for a moment then, Pembers."

The inspector briskly marched over to them, a frown etched on his forehead. He ignored the two dogs who greeted him and gave Churchill and Pemberley a disapproving shake of the head.

"It's not appropriate for you to be here," he stated. "This is a serious police matter. So serious in fact that Chief Inspector Llewellyn-Dalrymple will be joining us shortly."

"Joining us? You make it sound like a drinks party, Inspector."

"Which it most assuredly is not. Now can you leave the premises please while I conduct my investigations."

"But we've been asked by the family to investigate," responded Churchill, feeling a little smug.

He gave a groan.

"Yes I'm afraid so, Inspector. My dear friend, Miss Tryphena Ridley-Balls, has asked me to work on the case. We have her blessing. Perhaps we can work together?"

"There is no need for us to work together, Mrs Churchill."

"Why ever not? A problem shared is a problem halved, as they say."

"It's not something which the Compton Poppleford Constabulary routinely does."

"No, indeed, Inspector. Well, fortunately for you, we were just heading off anyway and we'll take all our notes and theories with us."

"Notes and theories?"

"Close the notebook, Pembers," hissed Churchill. "We don't want the inspector seeing all our notes and theories."

"But I've only written—"

"Close it!"

Pemberley did as she was told and the two ladies smiled sweetly at the police officer.

"Good luck, Inspector," said Churchill. "You'll need it, this is a tricky one."

Chapter 10

Churchill and Pemberley surveyed the incident board on their office wall the following day.

"It's rather early to consider suspects at this stage, but we certainly have a number of persons of interest, wouldn't you say, Pembers?"

"They're all suspects."

"I wouldn't say *all*." Churchill helped herself to a jam tart from a plate on Pemberley's desk. "Some are more suspicious than others. At the top of the list should surely be the people who were in the Earl's rooms on the day of his death. So that includes Mr Goldbeam and that ghoulish Mrs Surpant. Apparently Gertie the maid and Mr Porge were routine visitors too. So we have four possibilities."

"Not forgetting Tryphena and Cairistiona."

"We don't know if they were in his rooms on the day he died."

"But they're his daughters, they certainly would have had access to his rooms. They could have come and gone without raising anyone's suspicions whatsoever."

"Indeed. But Tryphena is hardly going to poison her own father is she?"

"Why not?"

"Because he's her father! And you've seen how upset she is by his death."

"Perhaps she's been shedding crocodile tears?"

"Oh Pemberley! What an awful thing to say about my dear friend!"

"Mrs Churchill, you can't allow your friendship with her to blinker your sensibilities."

"My sensibilities are far from blinkered!"

"Then you must consider her to be a person of interest. That's what a proper detective would do. That's what Atkins would have done."

"Well yes I suppose Mr Atkins, or perhaps I should call him Mr Perfect, would have considered anybody to be a person of interest. Even his own grandmother."

"It's true. He did actually once investigate his grandmother."

"Heartless."

"Not particularly, she stole a lot of money."

"Did she really? Golly."

"Anyone can commit a crime, Mrs Churchill. And, as you well know, it's often the ones you least expect."

"So you're suggesting that we should put my lovely friend, Tryph, on the incident board?"

"It has to be done."

"Oh cripes. She's going to be terribly upset by it. I don't think we should include her sister though, not yet. We don't know where she was on the day her father died."

"We should include Aunt Nora too."

"The ninety-seven year old lady in the bath chair?"

"Anyone is possible."

"Some much more possible than others. I think we

need to use a little common sense here, Pembers. It's immediately obvious that Mr Goldbeam is much more likely to have murdered the Earl than the elderly aunt confined to the top floor of the house."

"Atkins used to consider everyone until he could rule them out."

"Well, yes, that's what all good detectives do, including myself. Oh, is that someone on the stairs?"

The ladies turned to look at the doorway which Mrs Thonnings came trotting through just a moment later.

"Have you caught her red-handed yet?" she asked.

"Who?"

"Mrs Fancy-Pants. That Boutons and Ribbons lady, or whatever she calls herself."

"We haven't had a chance to yet, Mrs Thonnings, we've been tasked with an incredibly important murder investigation."

"Oh, the Earl." Mrs Thonnings sat herself down at Churchill's desk with a sigh. "What a shame my livelihood is less important than an old, deceased man."

"It's not a question of importance, Mrs Thonnings—"

"So why have you not managed to investigate yet, Mrs Churchill?"

"Well, it's a complicated case and we've spent some time discussing how we're going to approach it, haven't we Miss Pemberley?"

"Have we?"

"Yes we have. Now, the trouble with Mrs Bouton is that she's rather clever."

"No cleverer than me," grumbled Mrs Thonnings.

"No, you're clever too. But Mrs Bouton is wily and cunning."

"How do you know this?" asked Pemberley.

"I just know. I've met her and I'm a good judge of

character. And I also know that anyone clever enough to execute a poison pen letter campaign is clearly of sophisticated intelligence."

"Which means what?" asked Mrs Thonnings.

"Which means that Miss Pemberley and I must tread carefully. We must decide how we're going to investigate this without alerting Mrs Bouton to our intentions."

"And how do we do that?" asked Pemberley.

"Exactly. How? That's what we need to finish discussing."

"Did we even start discussing it?"

"Yes. Jam tart, Mrs Thonnings?"

"Thank you."

"So that's where we are," said Churchill, hoping that these words would mean the end of it and that she could now have a peaceful sit down with a cup of tea.

Mrs Thonnings shook her head sadly. "I saw Mrs Woolwell walk right past the shop yesterday. Normally she drops in to buy some buttons or a zip. Sometimes a reel of thread or a new needle for her sewing machine."

"Perhaps she didn't need any haberdashery supplies yesterday?"

"Oh she did all right. Because I tiptoed out of the shop and followed her."

"Goodness."

"And where do you think she went?"

"I don't know."

"Of course you know, Mrs Churchill! To Mrs Fancy-Pants that's where. And she was in there for a good ten minutes before coming out with a noticeably fuller shopping basket."

"Oh dear. Perhaps it's just the novelty of a new shop?"

"Yes," agreed Pemberley. "That's what it will be."

"Perhaps you could give your new shop a lick of paint, Mrs Thonnings?" suggested Churchill.

"Goodness, no. I can't afford it."

"Is there someone who could do it for you for a favour?"

"Well I would have once asked Mr Goldbeam but I can't ask now."

"Why not?"

"We parted on difficult terms."

"He was a man friend of yours?"

"Briefly. But anyway, that's water under the bridge now. I can't think of anyone who would paint my shop as a favour. What's really needed, Mrs Churchill, is for the author of those letters to be publicly unmasked. Then the newspaper will tell everyone what Mrs Fancy-Pants did and they'll all come back to my shop again. That's what needs to happen to resolve this!"

Chapter 11

"How are we going to prove that Mrs Bouton sent those letters about Mrs Thonnings to the *Compton Poppleford Gazette*?" Pemberley asked Churchill as the two ladies walked up the high street towards Boutons et Rubans with Oswald in tow.

"I don't know yet, Pembers. It's rather a puzzle. And, as much sympathy as I have for Mrs Thonnings' predicament, I rather wish that she hadn't asked us to investigate. I would like to be devoting all my energies to the Earl's murder. If Inspector Mappin solves it before we do then I shall be hopping mad."

"So what are you going to say to Mrs Bouton? Ask her outright about the letters?"

"Absolutely not, I think we just have to sniff about and get a feel for things."

"Which involves doing what, exactly?"

"It doesn't really entail an exact doing of anything. In these situations, I like to rely on my instincts and see where they lead me."

"Which means you haven't a clue how to go about it?"

"Of course I have a clue, Pembers! In this instance, we merely visit Mrs Bouton's shop and pretend that we're interested in her wares."

"Then see where our instincts lead us?"

"Exactly."

The ladies reached the lavender-fronted haberdashery shop and saw that its window display was even more enticingly arranged than on their previous visit.

"Mrs Bouton certainly has a way of displaying her wares, doesn't she Pembers?"

"She does. It makes me want to buy all these colourful reels of thread even though I hate sewing."

"Poor Mrs Thonnings." Churchill shook her head in dismay. "Mrs Bouton didn't even need to write all those nasty letters, just the act of opening this shop was enough to lure the customers away."

"Just look at that pin cushion. Have you ever seen anything like it?"

"Not outside of London."

"And look at those spools of braid! So intricately woven."

"Mrs Bouton clearly has a good supplier. I could do with some of those fabric scissors actually. Let's go inside."

"No dogs!" barked a voice as soon as they stepped through the door.

"Golly, she doesn't miss a trick, does she Pembers?" mumbled Churchill. Pemberley asked Oswald to sit outside and the two ladies surveyed the busy haberdashery shop. Buttons, ribbons, fabrics and thread were displayed in a rainbow of colours on meticulously arranged shelves and display stands. A pleasant perfume lingered in the air and a tranquil song drifted from a gramophone somewhere behind the counter.

"Oh hello, it's you two again!" said Mrs Bouton, her

thick, golden hair bouncing around her shoulders. "How lovely to see you! Are you looking for anything in particular?"

"We're just here for a little browse," replied Churchill.

"And I would like a yard of braid please," said Pemberley.

"What for?" asked Churchill.

"I don't know yet. I just like it."

Mrs Bouton gave a wide smile. "I know exactly what you mean, Miss Pemberley. It calls to you, doesn't it? My braid has been extremely popular, I fear that I might run out of it soon."

"In which case I'll take three yards of each type."

"Lovely!"

"Are you sure about this, Miss Pemberley?" queried Churchill.

"Absolutely sure," replied Pemberley as they watched Mrs Bouton unrolling and measuring out the braid.

Churchill whispered, "but she wouldn't even let Oswald in."

"Oh I don't mind about that, it's quite understandable. He'd probably only cause some mischief, you know what he's like."

Churchill shook her head in amazement, her assistant appeared to be under the spell of Boutons et Rubans.

"Oh hello, Mrs Churchill," said a woman with fair hair and protruding teeth. "Isn't this a wonderful new place?"

"Hello, Mrs Harris. Yes it is indeed."

"I can't stop coming here. We've needed a place like this in Compton Poppleford for some time."

"Have we? What about Mrs Thonnings' shop?"

"Oh yes, I'd forgotten about that! I seem to remember reading something about her in the newspaper. Someone blaming her for their drawers slipping down or something."

"Well it's not true."

"Is it not? Well you know what the newspapers are like these days, they'll print anything. Oh, look at the colour of that ribbon! I don't remember seeing that in here yesterday." Mrs Harris wandered off towards it, as if in a trance.

By now, Pemberley was counting out a number of coins and handing them to Mrs Bouton.

"Have you any elastic?" Churchill asked Mrs Bouton.

"Yes, it's just over there in the far corner. Are you after a particular type?"

"Elastic for a waistband."

"You're making a skirt?" Pemberley asked her.

"Yes." Churchill gave her assistant a surreptitious wink. "For a garden party I've been invited to in a few weeks. And I'd like to make sure that the waistband won't fail if I help myself to more sandwiches."

"Oh that was *you*, was it, Mrs Churchill?" asked Mrs Harris, her attention now diverted from the ribbon. "Cripes, how embarrassing for you." She called out across the shop. "Mrs Woolwell!"

"Yes?" came the reply from behind a display stand. "It was Mrs Churchill's skirt which fell down at the garden party!" continued Mrs Harris. "Do you remember we read about it in the newspaper?"

"Oh yes, how funny! Mrs Churchill, eh? What an embarrassment for her. Mind you, she always was the sort to go for second helpings."

"I'm right here, in case you hadn't noticed!" fumed Churchill. "And it wasn't me or my skirt!"

"But I thought you just said it was?" responded Mrs Harris.

"No. I wouldn't like it to happen to me which is why I

happened to mention it. I would like some elastic of the strongest strength."

"Well I can't say I blame you, Mrs Churchill. It would be quite upsetting for the vicar to see any more petticoats!"

"It's not the vicar I'm worried about, Mrs Harris. I wonder, Mrs Bouton, if you happened to read the news article about the recent elastic failures?"

Mrs Bouton pushed her lower lip out in a gesture of cluelessness and shook her head. "No, which article was that?"

"It was in the *Compton Poppleford Gazette*."

"And what's that?"

"The local newspaper."

"Never heard of it. I'm new to the village you see."

"Yes I realise that."

"I don't have time to read newspapers."

"Oh you'd have loved this particular news article, Mrs Bouton," said Mrs Harris. And she proceeded to tell the haberdasher about its contents. Churchill scrutinised the haberdasher's face as she listened, looking for a sign that she had knowledge of the letters. But, to Churchill's disappointment, she didn't give anything away.

"Goodness," she said, once Mrs Harris had finished her tale. "Well I can assure you, Mrs Churchill, that my elastic won't leave you red-faced."

"Jolly good."

"How much would you like?"

Churchill realised that it would seem rather odd if she now declined to buy any. "A yard, thank you."

"Will a yard be enough?" replied Mrs Bouton, eying her figure.

"More than enough thank you," she snapped. "Only part of the waistband will be elasticated."

. . .

"The cheek of the woman," muttered Churchill after the two ladies had left the shop and were walking down the high street to their office. "She's not exactly a strip of a lass herself."

"And she's either extremely good at lying or she had nothing to do with the letters sent to the *Compton Poppleford Gazette*," said Pemberley. "She showed barely a reaction at all!"

"She certainly has a face for poker. And I find her claim that she's never heard of the local newspaper rather hard to swallow."

"But she's a newcomer so I don't think it's completely unbelievable."

"No I suppose not. The question is, do we think she wrote those letters?"

"It's difficult to say. And I don't know how we can find out."

"Me neither. I must say that her performance so far has been impressive. Oh look, here comes Mrs Thonnings."

"You've been shopping?" commented their red-haired friend, once she was alongside them. "Those bags look like the ones from Mrs Fancy-Pants' shop."

"Well we've just been there investigating on your behalf, Mrs Thonnings. And we had to buy something otherwise it would appear rather obvious that we were just snooping."

"Miss Pemberley appears to have bought rather a lot."

"It's the braid, I couldn't resist it."

"I sell braid."

"Yes but this braid is different. There's something about the colours and the way it's woven—"

"Yes, thank you, Miss Pemberley," interrupted Churchill. "We don't need to go on about it. Mrs Thonnings, who's minding your shop while you're out and about?"

"No one, I've just put a sign up saying I'll be back in fifteen minutes."

"And what of your customers?"

"I don't have many these days."

"I'm not surprised if you keep closing your shop. You need to be there, Mrs Thonnings. And, while you're at it, you should try sprucing things up a little and rearranging your stock. You could even set up a gramophone to play some nice music."

"Are you telling me how to run my shop, Mrs Churchill?"

"No. But a lick of paint really would help as well."

"We've already discussed this."

"Mrs Thonnings, it's all very well asking for our help but you need to begin helping yourself too. Giving your shop a spring clean and actually keeping it open will work wonders. There's no point in us proving that Mrs Bouton sent those letters unless you put in a bit more effort. People are visiting her shop for a good reason and it's not entirely down to those letters."

Mrs Thonnings' lower lip began to wobble and her shoulders slumped. "Very well then. I'll go back to my shop."

Churchill felt a pang of guilt about the manner in which she'd just spoken to her.

"Well if you're on an important errand I'm sure another ten minutes or so won't do any harm."

"It will. You're quite right, Mrs Churchill. I need to go back to my shop now. I'll see if I can find someone who'll paint it too. Perhaps Mr Goldbeam might take pity on me, but I doubt it."

She turned away and began to head off.

"Oh don't be sad, Mrs Thonnings!" Churchill called out after her. "We can sort this out, I feel sure of it!"

Her friend acknowledged her with a sad wave and went on her way.

"Oh dear, now I've upset her," said Churchill.

"It was quite a telling off."

"I didn't mean it to be. I feel so terribly awful about it now. Do you think she'll forgive me?"

Pemberley gave a shrug. "Only if you can prove Mrs Bouton is behind the letters."

"Oh darn it! Let's go and buy some extra supplies from the bakery."

Chapter 12

"I WORKED for the late Earl of Middlemop for twenty-two years," announced Mr Porge. "I carried out the role of both butler and personal valet."

"So you were quite busy?"

"Indeed."

Churchill observed how the man's face barely moved when he spoke. His deadpan expression and unblinking eyes were characteristic of a person who'd served a lifetime of dutiful subjugation. Mr Porge looked to be about fifty years of age. He was long-faced: a feature exacerbated by his high-perched eyebrows and a jaw which hung low while his mouth remained closed, resulting in the corners of his mouth being perpetually pulled down.

They sat in the library, a room made gloomy by the countless dark leather volumes which lined its walls. Churchill surmised that if the Earl had enjoyed reading, he hadn't particularly enjoyed reading anything cheery.

"May I ask when you last saw your employer alive?" she asked.

"It was after he had dined that evening."

"And what time was that?"

"Seven o'clock."

Churchill glanced at Pemberley to see if she was writing anything down, but she wasn't.

"Mrs Surpant told us that he dined in his rooms, is that correct?"

"Yes."

"So you were in his rooms with him at that time?"

"Yes."

"Was seven o'clock the usual time you knocked off for the day?"

"My duties would typically end at about that time. If he had an evening appointment, which was unusual in his later years, I would attend to his requisite needs. Latterly, it was quite usual for me to finish my work at seven o'clock in the evening."

"Good."

Pemberley stifled a yawn.

The butler was so dull, stiff and immobile that Churchill was tempted to lean forward and tickle him, just to elicit a more interesting response.

"And what final duties did you carry out for your employer that evening?" she asked.

"I laid his pyjamas out on his bed, turned down the coverlet and put some more coal on the fire. He then went into the bathroom to perform his ablutions."

"You left while he was in the bathroom?"

"Yes, the Earl liked to ready himself for bed. He was capable of doing so and didn't require assistance."

"Good."

"Making a silly fuss is how he described it."

"Described what exactly?"

"Assistance of any sort. He called it making a silly fuss."

"Great. And how was he when you left him to perform his ablutions?"

"His usual self."

"Which was what?"

"A little cantankerous but in good spirits. As much as one can expect from a man of his age." He glanced over at the window and said, "is that your dog out there?"

Churchill followed his gaze to the lawn where Oswald frolicked with Margery.

"He belongs to Miss Pemberley."

"Well tell him he can't dig any holes on the front lawn."

"We'll be sure to do that. Now, when you left the Earl's rooms, he was performing his ablutions. It was shortly after that when he consumed the fatal dose of Dr Crumpot's Remedy Syrup?"

"I believe that to be the case, yes."

"And the next person who saw him after that was Gertie?"

"Yes, except he was dead by then."

"Of course. And where were you when you heard the sad news?"

"I was dining in the servants' kitchen with Mrs Surpant. Gertie had gone to the Earl's rooms to collect his supper tray but swiftly dashed downstairs empty-handed to summon us. She had such a look of alarm upon her face that we both rose from the table in an instant. Mrs Surpant dashed off first but I'm a little slower because of my leg. Once I got upstairs, I encountered the housekeeper in the corridor outside the Earl's rooms and her face was as white as a sheet."

"And did you go to see the Earl?"

"I did."

"And where did you find him?"

"He was on his bed. Lying across it as though he'd succumbed to an attack of some sort and fell onto the bed in a haphazard fashion. He hadn't yet put on his pyjamas."

"Goodness."

"The effects were rather swift you see."

"So I understand. Have you any idea who could have put the poison in his remedy syrup?"

"No idea at all."

"Did you see anyone suspicious in or near his rooms during that day or early evening?"

"No. I would have apprehended them if I had."

"Of course."

Churchill glanced at Pemberley and noticed that her eyelids were becoming heavy.

"There is something rather unnatural that I should add," said the butler.

Pemberley's eyes opened wide.

"Unnatural?" queried Churchill.

"Yes, I refuse to believe the stories of the various hauntings in this place, however…"

"Yes?"

"There was another reason Mrs Surpant was so white-faced."

"A ghost?"

He gave a solemn nod. "She told me that she'd just seen the grey lady."

"Oh goodness, really? The portent of death?"

He gave another nod. "I don't usually pay heed to such nonsense, but on this occasion…"

Churchill gave a shiver and glanced at her assistant whose face was frozen in a painful grimace.

"Mrs Surpant was clearly in shock at the time," said Churchill with forced cheer. "Her nerves would have been deeply affected."

"I agree," replied the butler.

"You do? Oh good. So there you go you see, Miss Pemberley, no need to worry."

Pemberley swallowed and gave a weak smile. Churchill decided to lighten the mood and exact a livelier response from the butler, it would be interesting to find out if he was capable of expressing more than one emotion.

"What do you do when you have some time off, Mr Porge?"

"I don't see why that question is relevant to the death of the Earl of Middlemop."

"I'm just interested."

"May I ask why?"

"I'm interested in all the people we're speaking to in the course of our investigation. Perhaps you could tell me what you do when you have some time off?"

He cleared his throat awkwardly. "Erm, I like to fish. And every Thursday evening I take the train to Dorchester and go to the pictures."

"The pictures, eh? And what do you enjoy watching there?"

"I don't see why that matters, Mrs Churchill."

"I'm merely making conversation. I realise you're a professional, Mr Porge, but you're also a human being with emotions and impulses too, I dare say. I'm under no doubt at all that you must relax a little when you're off duty. Surely the Mr Porge who is encountered below stairs is quite different to the Mr Porge above stairs?" She gave him a playful wink and noticed his face colour.

"I'm just the butler and valet," he responded curtly. "And I find these questions rather too personal in nature if I may say so."

"I do apologise if I have offended you Mr Porge, I'm merely interested in understanding a little more about you,

you see. It's the role of a detective to learn about the motivations of people."

"I have told you all that is relevant, Mrs Churchill. I don't see why my personal hobbies and interests are of any relevance to your investigation." He got to his feet. "Now, I must be getting on with my work if you'll excuse me."

"Of course. Thank you for your time, Mr Porge. We may need to speak to you again if that's all right."

"I don't have anything else to tell you."

And with these words he left the room.

"Oh, now he's slipped through our fingers!" lamented Churchill. "I so desperately wanted to ruffle him, Pembers! I want to chisel away at that granite exterior and discover what lies beneath."

"Ugh, really?"

"Yes, really! Don't you have the urge to do the same?"

"Not an enormous urge to, no."

"Beneath that stiffly starched shirt front lies the beating heart of a man, Pembers."

"I don't want to consider what's beneath Mr Porge's shirt, Mrs Churchill, and I'm surprised that you do because the man hasn't an ounce of charm."

"He's not supposed to have any, Pembers, he's a butler. A butler with something to hide I'd say. Don't you see how he's the perfect candidate for having poisoned the Earl? While the old boy was gobbling up his supper, Porge could quite easily have nipped into the bathroom and popped some cyanide into his remedy syrup. He knew the Earl took a good dose of it each evening before retiring. And then he dashed off before the death throes. Rather convenient wouldn't you say?"

"As well as cruel and cold-hearted."

"Certainly. That's why I wanted to try and shake him

up a little. Get a reaction from him. Something. Anything! Have you ever met a person as sombre and dour as him?"

"Mrs Surpant."

"That's true. Between them, they're quite a pair aren't they? I wonder why the Earl employed such miserable servants."

"Well I never met the man, but he doesn't appear to have been a bundle of laughs himself."

"I don't disagree with you there, Pembers. Now let's go and find that maid Gertie. I'm sure she will have something interesting to tell us."

Chapter 13

"You may have Gertie for ten minutes," announced Mrs Surpant once she had escorted the maid to the library. "And after that, she's required in the pantry to repaper the shelves."

"Just ten minutes?" queried Churchill.

"You're lucky to even have that. We're busy today."

She turned on her heel and Churchill watched her dark form glide away. "Never mind," she muttered, "it's just as well we're not carrying out an important murder investigation." Gertie gave a conspiratorial giggle. She was a young, stout woman with a chubby face and smiling eyes.

"We're so sorry to hear about the demise of your employer," said Churchill as the maid sat down with them. "It must have been extremely distressing for you to find him as you did."

"It didn't bother me too much, truth be told. Was just like when I found me grandad all sprawled out by 'is fire-place. That's the thing with old blokes, ain't it? They just go all of a sudden. Just like that."

"I suppose they can do. Although in this case, of course, the Earl was poisoned."

"Yeah, that's a bit strange ain't it? Dunno why someone bothered with that."

"Have you any idea who it could have been?"

"None."

"Anyone with a grudge against him?"

"Well I s'pose they must have 'ad a grudge if they went 'n' poisoned him."

"A point well made! Anyone you know of who bore a grudge?"

"No, no one I know of."

"Any of the servants perhaps?"

"No, why would a servant do it?"

"I don't know, that's what I'm asking you. Miss Pemberley and I are as baffled as you are."

"So that makes three of us then. Best leave it to the police I say."

"Not necessarily. Miss Pemberley and I have been tasked by Miss Ridley-Balls to find out who murdered her father."

"How you gonna do that then?"

"Well that's a good question, Gertie. Have you got any information at all which might be helpful to us?"

"All I can tell you is what I saw that day, Mrs Churchill. I took 'is lordship's dinner up and Mr Porge was up there 'n' all."

"Was that usual?"

"Yeah."

"It was the same as any other evening, would you say?"

"Yeah, I would say. So I took 'is dinner up, put the tray on the table by the fire then I left."

"What time was that?"

"Six o'clock like it always was."

"And what were the two gentlemen doing at the time?"

"His lordship was mutterin' something about specks of ash on his writin' table and Mr Porge was hangin' something in the wardrobe."

"Specks of ash on the writing table?"

"Yeah, his lordship was sayin' there was specks of ash and that someone 'adn't been dustin' in there proper. Well, knowin' it was me what dusted in there last, I scarpered quick. I was waitin' for Mrs Surpant to pull me up on it later. I knew that was the next thing that he'd do, he'd go complainin' to 'er about the specks of ash."

"Did you see these specks of ash?"

"Nah, I scarpered, fully expectin' I'd 'ave to sort it the followin' day. I weren't lookin' forward to collecting 'is supper tray 'cos I was expectin' 'im to start going on about the specks of ash again."

"And when you went to collect the tray you discovered him dead?"

"Yeah, all sprawled out just like me grandad. Only he was on his bed. Just fallen on it, like." Gertie slumped her shoulders, held out her arms and pushed her tongue out in a demonstration of someone who was insensible.

"Golly. It must have been quite upsetting."

"I just ran out o' there and fetched Mrs Surpant and Mr Porge. Let them deal with it all."

"And this was at what time?"

"About eight o'clock."

"When you delivered the Earl's dinner, did you notice Mr Porge in or near the bathroom?"

"Nah, he had 'is head in the wardrobe."

"And are you familiar with the remedy syrup which the Earl took?"

"Dr Crumpot's? Yeah, it was me job to fetch it from the pharmacy."

"Was it indeed? Interesting."

"Once a month I collected it. Jonny from the stables took me down in the pony and trap, there was a lot o'bottles to bring back you see."

"And have you any idea how someone could have put cyanide in the remedy syrup?"

"Well they must have gone in there and done it when no one was lookin'."

"Good point. Is it possible that the bottle in the bathroom was swapped for one which contained poison, do you think?"

She gave this some thought. "S'pose it is."

"Where were the bottles of Dr Crumpot's Remedy Syrup stored?"

"In a chest in the pantry. It was my job to fetch a new one when I noticed the bottle in 'is bathroom gettin' low."

"Very interesting. How often did you check the bottle in the bathroom?"

"Most days."

"And you checked the bottle of remedy syrup on the day the Earl died?"

"Yeah, I checked it in the mornin'. It was about three quarters full."

"Can you recall what the level had been the previous day?"

"Would have been a bit more than that."

"But can you specifically recall what it was?"

There was a pause as Gertie crumpled her face, deep in thought. "Nah," she said eventually. "I can't exactly remember what it was. But when I checked it on the mornin' he died, I weren't surprised by the level what was in it, if that makes sense. It weren't as if it were almost empty the day before and then it was suddenly three quarters full. I would've noticed that."

"I see. So it wasn't a new bottle which had been placed there?"

"Nah."

"And it didn't appear to have been topped up?"

"Nah."

"The amount of medicine in the bottle was what you had expected it to be?"

"Yeah."

"Gertie, you have been enormously helpful."

"Have I?" She sat back in her chair with an appreciative grin. "Really?"

"Yes, very helpful indeed."

"Well I'll be blowed! I'll 'ave to tell me ma that the nice lady detectives said I was very helpful!"

"Yes you can tell your mother that if you like."

A dark figure appeared in the library doorway.

"Looks like you have to go and repaper the pantry shelves now Gertie," said Churchill, reluctant to make eye contact with the ghoulish housekeeper.

"Yeah. I'll be on me way. Thank you for a lovely chat."

"Well what a nice lass," said Churchill once Gertie had departed with the housekeeper.

"She could still be a murderer though," said Pemberley.

"Yes I realise we can't rule anyone out just yet. But I can't imagine her poisoning the Earl."

"She had the perfect opportunity to."

"When? Mr Porge was present when she took the Earl's dinner up."

"But what about when she collected the tray? She could have put the poison in the Earl's remedy syrup then."

89

"So you don't think she discovered him dead after all?"

"We can't prove it either way yet, can we? He could have been alive and well when she went to collect the tray. Perhaps she then went into the bathroom, put the cyanide into his medicine bottle and then helped him take the dose?"

"Golly. We can't prove she didn't do that."

"She doesn't seem to be particularly upset by his passing, does she?"

"Well I can only assume she didn't like him very much."

"And it was her job to collect the bottles of remedy syrup from the pharmacy and check the level of the medicine in the bottle each day. If anyone swapped his bottle with one which had been poisoned then Gertie is the most likely candidate."

"Oh don't be so down on Gertie, Pembers, she's about the only person I like so far. Apart from dear Tryph of course."

"She had the best opportunity to poison him."

"Ah, but what could her motive have been eh, Pembers? Answer me that."

"I don't know."

"There we go then."

"But then again we haven't found anyone with a motive yet, have we?"

"Hello ladies!" Tryphena bustled into the room and Churchill felt immediately worried that she might have been listening to their conversation from the corridor.

"Tryph! What a surprise!"

"How are you getting on?"

"Quite well actually, we've chatted with Mr Porge and Gertie today."

"Jolly good. Any theories yet?"

"Not yet, we need to speak to everyone before we can start on those. I realise she doesn't like impromptu visitors, Tryphena, but please may we speak to your Aunt Nora?"

"She's a little bit batty."

"Well so am I."

"And confused."

"Snap."

"I'll go and speak with her nurse and see what she says. She may ask you to come back in a few days."

"Which is all very well Tryph, but if you want us to come up with some theories then we'll need to speak to her as soon as possible."

"Very well, I shall go and find out for you. She might be asleep of course. She sleeps a lot."

"Can you please find out?"

Tryphena sighed. "All right then."

Chapter 14

A SHORT WHILE LATER, Tryphena escorted Churchill and Pemberley up a staircase to the top storey of the house.

"Has your Aunt Nora lived here all her life?" asked Churchill.

"Only since her husband died."

"So not terribly long, then?"

"It's about sixty-two years since Mr Ponsonby-Staithes passed."

"So it has been a long time then."

"Yes, I suppose it is when you think about it. Funny, really. I can just about remember Uncle Gerald. They were quite a pair back then, they both loved a song and a dance. Aunt Nora is ninety-seven now so I don't know what you'll get out of her. She's chatty some days and sleepy on others. She absolutely detests any change in her routine and she's not keen on strangers either so I think her nurse is doing her best to prepare her for your visit."

They reached the top of the staircase.

"Your poor Aunt Nora having to be carried up and

down these stairs," commented Churchill. "Perhaps there may be an opportunity for that to change now."

"It depends on who inherits the house," replied Tryphena.

"Surely it's the grandson isn't it? Humphrey Ridley-Balls?"

"Possibly. We shall find out on Tuesday."

"You appear to be rather laissez-faire about who inherits the Gripedown Estate, Tryphena."

"I wouldn't describe it as that, Annabel. But I really don't mind you see. I've long accepted that the house won't be mine."

"That it will go to Humphrey Ridley-Balls?"

"Possibly. Not that it should."

"Why do you say that, Tryph? If he's the heir in the eyes of the law, then isn't it to be expected?"

"Daddy was always full of surprises."

"Was he? In what way?"

"Many ways. Here we are." Tryphena stopped at a door in the corridor and rested her hand on the doorknob. "Aunt Nora's rooms. Now, her nurse tells me she's just woken up so don't make any sudden movements or unexpected noises."

"Aunt Nora or the nurse?"

"Aunt Nora. Oh I see, you were joking just then?"

"It wasn't terribly funny was it? Do carry on."

"Right. You'll need to sit on her left side so she can hear you properly. And, although it's tempting to speak loudly in case you think she can't hear you, she doesn't like loud voices so a normal volume is fine."

"Rightyo."

"If she turns away from you, she's had enough."

"I can understand that feeling."

"If she nods off, please just leave her be. Don't try to wake her up again as that will startle her."

"I can understand that feeling too."

"She's not allowed sweets as they make her excitable."

"I don't have any of those on me. Do you have any sweets in your handbag, Miss Pemberley?"

Her assistant shook her head.

"She doesn't like to be touched, she gets very upset about that."

"I have no intention of doing so."

"Some people are tempted to tap her on the arm, hand or shoulder, she absolutely hates it."

"I'll be doing nothing of the sort." Churchill's eyes darted impatiently to the hand on the doorknob. "Can we go in now, Tryphena?"

"I just need to establish these rules with you, Annabel. She's very old."

"We're not exactly spring chickens ourselves, Tryphena. If anyone is any good at managing old people then it's other old people."

"If you say so. But do be careful with her."

"Does she bite?"

"No she doesn't bite, fortunately. So there's no need to worry about that."

"I was joking with you again, Tryphena."

"Oh."

"Now please let us speak to your aunt before she goes off to sleep again."

"Of course."

They stepped into a large, comfortable room where the settees, chairs and a day bed were all covered with blankets and cushions. The scent of rose water hung in the air. A wicker bath chair was positioned by a set of windows which had a commanding view of the gardens at the rear of the house. Within the bath chair sat a small figure, huddled beneath blankets and a wide-brimmed straw hat. As they began to approach the bath chair, a large-bosomed lady in a starched nurse's uniform stepped into view.

"Hello," she said. "I've prepared Mrs Ponsonby-Staithes as much as I possibly can for your visit but do excuse her as she can be a little rude when she's just woken up."

"From what I've heard about Mrs Ponsonby-Staithes so far, we have a great deal in common," said Churchill.

"Well I shall leave you in Nellie's capable hands, Annabel," said Tryphena. "Now I must go and attend to some papers of Daddy's."

"Of course."

Tryphena went on her way and the nurse placed two chairs to the left of the bath chair before settling herself on one of the settees with a book in hand. Churchill and Pemberley exchanged a cautious glance before positioning themselves next to the old lady. She didn't acknowledge them at first, instead peering down at the view of the gardens. Churchill wondered if she wished she was out there. Then, as they waited for the old lady to acknowledge them, Churchill wondered if she was capable of thinking much at all.

"Hello Mrs Ponsonby-Staithes, we've come to ask you a few questions if that's all right."

"So you do speak after all," replied Aunt Nora, now turning to them. "I was wondering if you'd been struck dumb." Sharp green eyes peered at them from her heavily-lined face and the brim of her hat rested on large, protruding ears.

"Oh yes, it's a pleasure to meet you."

"You're the two detective ladies."

"That's right. Please do accept our condolences on the sad passing of your brother."

Aunt Nora gave a tut. "Oh, him."

"Did you see him before he died?"

"Lots of times!"

"I meant recently."

"Not that recently, no. Not since I've got stuck with this thing." She slammed a veined hand on the arm of her bath chair.

"I'm sorry to hear that."

"Oh it's not a problem at all. My brother and I were acquainted for ninety-seven years and had pretty much said all that we needed to say to each other a long time ago. In fact I detested the man."

"I see. Is it a recent thing, your bath chair?" Churchill asked.

"Quite recent, yes. About three months I think."

"How frustrating for you."

"Fit as a fiddle I was and then suddenly, well it all just comes to an end, doesn't it?"

"Not an actual end I hope."

"Well that's going to happen before long. And some-times I get so terribly confused. I'm lucid at the present time."

"So I see."

"And then a fog descends on me and I don't know whether I'm coming or going and spout all sorts of nonsense. I'm quite aware of it but there's not a great deal I can do about it. Never grow old Mrs Churchill!"

"Well I fear I may be disobeying you there, Mrs Ponsonby-Staithes."

"Anyway, I'm quite comfortable up here these days, I did have a few rats for company but his lordship got rid of them."

"Ugh! Rats?"

"Oh I don't mind them, it was quite entertaining when they scrambled up the curtains. Anyway, his lordship put an end to that bit of fun."

"I must say that I agree with him on that front."

"Other than that, I'm quite content. Nellie brings me everything I need and I don't have to speak to people very often."

"Apart from us, I'm sorry about that."

"Why are you apologising?" She glanced at the two ladies with a little more interest now. "I was a lady detective once myself."

"Gosh, really?"

"Oh yes. I set up a small practice in London and spent my time trailing unfaithful spouses. I was involved in quite a few divorce cases in my day."

"Crikey."

"In fact that's how I met my husband. He asked me to follow his wife to Paris because he suspected she'd gone there with her French lover."

"And had she?"

"Yes. So I went back and told him as such and that rather sealed matters. I gave evidence in the court room, the divorce was granted and a year later we were married."

"Cripes, what a story."

"Then he died two years later."

"Oh dear, how awful."

"I didn't have the same enthusiasm for detective work after that so I came back here to the family home and annoyed my brother for the remaining sixty odd years."

"Time well spent then."

"It certainly was. So what do you want to ask me?"

"If there's anyone you know of who could possibly wish to poison your brother."

"No idea at all. Someone wouldn't exactly be vocal about their plans to do so, would they?"

"No. But there may have been someone he'd crossed swords with shortly before his death."

"I'm sure there was, but I couldn't tell you anything about it because I've been spending my time stuck up here."

"I see." Churchill searched her mind for something else to ask the old lady. Her mind was sharper than Churchill had anticipated. "It will be interesting to discover the contents of your brother's will, don't you think?"

Aunt Nora tutted again. "Not especially."

"Don't you want to find out what he's left you?"

"Not really. What use would I have for it now?"

"Perhaps you might like to be reassured that your final years will be lived out in this magnificent place?"

"Well they will be. There aren't many of them left and I can't imagine anyone being able to force me to leave."

"The rightful heir is Humphrey Ridley-Balls, is that right?"

"Yes, he's supposedly the heir."

"I understand, Mrs Ponsonby-Staithes, that there's a little kerfuffle about Humphrey, as if he's somehow not deserving of the family fortune."

"Ah." The old lady gave a smile. "Thereby hangs a tale."

"So I hear! Would you care to share it?"

"How long have you got?"

"All the time in the world!" responded Churchill, deciding that she was increasingly warming to Aunt Nora. "Isn't that right, Miss Pemberley?"

"I suppose so."

"Nellie!" called out the old lady, "ask Gertie to bring us

up some tea and cakes. Mrs Churchill and Miss Pemberley will be here for a little while."

Churchill now began to wonder if she actually preferred Aunt Nora to Tryphena. "Ready yourself with your notebook, Miss Pemberley," she said with a wink. "It looks like we're about to be regaled."

Chapter 15

GERTIE BROUGHT up the tea tray and laid out the teapot, cups, plates and cakes. Churchill tucked into a slice of walnut cake and decided that murder investigations could occasionally be quite fun.

"So Humphrey Ridley-Balls," she ventured, wiping cake crumbs from her mouth with a serviette. "No one seems to speak particularly highly of him."

"There's a reason for that," replied Aunt Nora.

"Well I've come to the conclusion that there could be. Would you be able to furnish me with particulars?"

"Indeed. Don't you think it's funny how he has three older sisters?"

"It doesn't strike me as particularly amusing."

"I didn't mean funny in that way. Funny as in…" She leant forwards a little and raised her wispy eyebrows. "Mysterious."

"Is it mysterious?"

"It is when you consider where he was born."

"Which was where?"

"In a little basket weaver's cottage by the River Turnfork."

"Which is where?"

"Oh a long way away from here." The old lady gave a dismissive wave of the hand.

"Where exactly?"

"Over the other side of the Brandleford Downs."

"I have no idea where that is, I'm afraid. I've not been a Dorset resident for long."

"The Brandleford Downs are about six miles from here," said Pemberley.

"So Humphrey Ridley-Balls was born a long way away from here, about six miles?"

"No, much more remote than that," said Aunt Nora. "The Turnfork river runs the other side of the Downs from here so the basket weaver's cottage is about seven miles away."

"Right. A tad unusual for the child of a wealthy family to be born in a basket wearer's cottage, wouldn't you say?"

"Ah ha!" The old lady cackled. "You've cottoned on, Mrs Churchill!" She gave her a toothy grin.

"Have I? Actually I don't think I have."

"The three sisters were all born at Loxley Grange," said Aunt Nora. "The home of Horace Ridley-Balls. It's what you'd expect, isn't it?"

"Indeed."

"But Master Humphrey was born at the cottage."

"Yes. Why?"

"Well the story we've all been told is that his father, Horace, and mother, Delilah, decided to take a long walk to bring on the birth."

"I see."

"But the long walk turned out longer than expected because they got lost."

"Oh dear."

"Lost in Berringdales Forest. They took a wrong turn and found themselves right in the middle of it. And dusk was coming and all the creatures of the night were emerging from their dens."

Churchill gave a shiver. "Now I wouldn't like that at all."

"They were cold, they were afraid," continued Aunt Nora. "Night fell and they couldn't see anything except for shining eyes staring at them from between the trees."

"Well that really does sound unpleasant."

"Hopelessly lost they were! On and on they walked and there was no sight nor sound of another living person! And then they began hearing a strange howling noise. Howww-wooooool!"

Churchill startled. "Good grief, Mrs Ponsonby-Staithes! You quite surprised me there!"

"Howwwwooooool!" She followed this with a mischievous chuckle.

"Can we skip on to the basket weaver's cottage?"

"Skip on? What do you want to skip on for?"

"I'd quite like to get to the main event of the story, the birth of Humphrey Ridley-Balls."

Aunt Nora pushed her lower lip out and adjusted her hat. "I can skip on if you want, but you'll miss some of the story."

"I don't mind that."

"You don't?"

"I do," said Pemberley. "What was making the howling noise?"

"They never found out."

"There you go, Miss Pemberley. Hardly worth asking, was it?"

"Some things are best left as a mystery," said Aunt Nora.

Churchill began to grow impatient. "Presumably what happened next is that Mr and Mrs Ridley-Balls happened across a cottage by the river and sought shelter there? And then, during the night, little Master Ridley-Balls put in an appearance?"

"Yes," replied the old lady sullenly. "Have you heard this one before?"

"No I haven't, I just guessed it. Which wasn't too difficult to be frank with you. Did the family return back to Loxley Grange the following day?"

"Yes, the basket weaver took them home in his pony and trap."

"So the reason no one speaks highly of Humphrey Ridley-Balls is because he was born in lowly surroundings?"

"It's not just that, Mrs Churchill."

"So what is it?"

Aunt Nora's eyes grew wide. "He's a changeling!"

"Golly, really?"

"The story I've just told you, although I'm rather annoyed you forced me to skip some of it, is the story that Mr and Mrs Ridley-Balls told everyone when they returned to Loxley Grange with their newly born son."

"The newly born son who was a changeling?"

"Exactly, Mrs Churchill! Mr and Mrs Ridley-Balls had three girls, there's no telling how desperate they were for a baby boy! Don't you think it odd that they went off to the forest and came back with a baby boy? Now why wasn't he born at Loxley Grange, do you suppose?"

"Because they went for a long walk and got lost."

"A convincing story isn't it? Now suppose they went off to the forest to fetch him?"

"He wasn't their child?"

"No, he was a changeling!"

"Don't changelings have something do with fairies? I can't believe we could be discussing such nonsense."

"Fairies if that's what you believe in, Mrs Churchill. But the story goes that the basket weaver's wife gave birth to a son that same night while Mrs Ridley-Balls gave birth to a daughter. It's said they either agreed to swap the two babies or the Ridley-Balls switched them when the basket weavers weren't looking?"

"How would they manage that?"

She shrugged. "I don't know. But it's said that, after the Ridley-Balls returned from the forest, the basket weavers were never seen again."

"It's said or it's true?"

She shrugged again. "There's another twist you can put on this too. Perhaps Mrs Ridley-Balls was never actually with child, perhaps she just put cushions up her dress because she was planning to buy the basket weavers' baby? It could have been a pre-arranged agreement between the four of them, the Ridley-Balls' could have paid good money for the baby."

"And if it had turned out to be a girl?" asked Pemberley.

"I don't know what they would have done then."

"I fear this story is a little far-fetched," said Churchill.

"They needed an heir!"

"Was the basket weaver's wife definitely with child?"

"I don't know, I never set eyes on her."

"But it is possible that Mrs Ridley-Balls gave birth to Humphrey in the basket weaver's cottage."

"It is possible, I grant you that. But why did the Ridley-Balls go there? Something's not right about that boy, Humphrey, he's got a look of the fairies about him."

"I can't see what it has to do with fairies. Does he look like Mr and Mrs Basket Weaver? That would be a clue."

"I don't know, they vanished."

Churchill sat back in her chair and helped herself to another slice of walnut cake. "I think it's a wonderful story, Mrs Ponsonby-Staithes, but I also think it's a tall tale."

The old lady sniffed. "You can think that if you like."

"And what do you think? After all, you're Humphrey Ridley-Balls's great aunt."

"If he's a true Ridley-Ball I am."

"And is he a true Ridley-Ball?"

"I like to believe he's a changeling because it's a more interesting story, don't you think?"

"Yes it is more interesting. But if he's a changeling, should he inherit Gripedown Hall?"

"Absolutely not!"

"Then who should it be?"

"I have lots of theories, Mrs Churchill."

"Would you care to share any of them?"

"No."

"Oh."

"And I'll tell you why." The old lady leant forward and pointed a crooked finger at Churchill. "I think you're a very astute lady Mrs Churchill, if you're half as good a detective as I ever was then you'll work it out for yourself."

Chapter 16

"Now I UNDERSTAND why Tryph has been so sniffy about her nephew, Humphrey," said Churchill, as the two ladies and their dog travelled back to the village in Mr Speakman's taxi.

"Well I think it's a load of nonsense," said Pemberley.

"There could be some truth in it."

"How?"

"Well it's rather odd that they decided to take such a long walk shortly before the baby was born, isn't it?"

"She was trying to make things come about. And come about they did."

"But what of the suggestion that she wasn't even with child? The Ridley-Balls could have paid the basket weavers a vast sum of money for the baby."

"I've never been a parent but I can't imagine ever selling my child."

"Some people do I'm afraid, Pembers."

"Such as who?"

"The basket weavers maybe?"

"Have you ever known anyone else do it?"

"No, but you hear of it."

"When?"

"I can't recall specifics at this very moment, Pembers, but you certainly hear of it. A poverty stricken family selling their child. They do it reluctantly of course, but all they want is a better life for their offspring. Humphrey has probably led a charmed existence with his inordinately wealthy family."

"They'd have packed him off to boarding school as soon as he could speak."

"Well it would have been charming before then, no doubt. And charming when he was home in the holidays."

"I think I'd prefer to live in a little cottage by a river than a big old draughty house with hordes of servants everywhere."

"But that's just you, Pembers. Personally I wouldn't have turned my nose up at being brought up in a stately home with tennis courts and ponies and boats to lark about in."

"I'm sure it sounds better than it actually is. If you'd been born into that world, your parents would have put great expectation upon you. You wouldn't have been allowed to marry Detective Chief Inspector Churchill, instead you would have been betrothed to a toffee-nosed youth called Tarquin de Montford or something like that."

"I've noticed before that you can be terribly disparaging about the upper classes, Pembers. There's really no need for it. You must remember that I'm a distant relative of the Duke of Marlborough nonetheless."

"You've managed to find a family line which connects you?"

"Not exactly. But the clue's in the name, don't you think? The Spencer-Churchills."

"Your husband's name."

"Yes. Anyway, as usual, we've strayed so far from the topic that I fear it's almost lost to us. What was it again? Ah yes the story of baby Humphrey and the basket weavers."

"Well I think it's one of those silly old village stories."

"You could be right, Pembers. But shall we keep an open mind? I've learned never to dismiss anything outright."

Chapter 17

THE FOLLOWING DAY, Churchill and Pemberley stood outside the green-fronted pharmacy on the high street. Sloped gold lettering above the window spelled out the name: 'Pollit & Pollit'.

"I've only encountered one Pollit in this place, Pembers. Have you ever seen the other one?"

"Now that you come to mention it, I haven't."

"I wonder what happened to him? Or possibly her."

"Maybe nothing happened to them? Perhaps they work in the back room all the time?"

"That's a good point, perhaps they do. One Pollit out the back and the other out the front. Well let's make some enquiries and, if we're lucky, we could end up speaking to both of them. Ask Oswald to wait politely for us out here."

"I'll try."

A strong medicinal smell greeted the two ladies as they stepped inside the pharmacy. Glass display cabinets held countless bottles, packets and boxes. More were stacked up on the mahogany counter and hundreds of little wooden drawers covered the walls.

"Good morning ladies." A bespectacled face peered over a row of medicine bottles.

"Good morning Mr Pollit." The face vanished again. "Mr Pollit?"

"Yes?"

"Good grief, how did you get over there?"

The pharmacist sidled smugly out from behind a mahogany cabinet as if he had just won a game of hide and seek. His oiled hair was neatly parted and he wore a pristine white coat.

"Surprised you, did I?"

"Yes."

"Perhaps you need help with your nerves, Mrs Churchill? I can suggest a good remedy."

"I'm sure you can, Mr Pollit, however my nerves are quite satisfactory thank you. Now, my assistant and I are here on an investigative matter. You've heard about the awful murder of the Earl of Middlemop, I take it?"

"I certainly have, awful indeed."

"Churchill's Detective Agency has been tasked with finding the culprit."

"Gosh, good luck with that, Mrs Churchill."

"We hear you're the purveyor of medicines to the Ridley-Balls household, I expect Inspector Mappin has already been in here sniffing about."

"It was one of his constables actually. He asked me a few questions."

"About the dyspepsia medication which was poisoned with cyanide?"

"Yes, but the cyanide had nothing to do with me. I made that clear to him. I managed to sell him three boxes of liver pills too. I could tell by his gait that he needed some relief."

"Jolly good. How long did you supply Dr Crumpot's

Remedy Syrup to the Earl for?"

"Oh at least ten years. Probably more."

"I believe Gertie the maid was sent down here to collect the stuff—"

"Stuff? You can't describe Dr Crumpot's Remedy Syrup as mere *stuff* you know."

"Well the medicine, then."

"It's more than mere medicine, Mrs Churchill, it's a life-changing elixir!"

"Good, well I—"

"It straightens the back!"

"Really?"

"And brightens the eye! It restores the complexion and strengthens the muscular system."

"Good."

"It prevents the clogging up of nature's drainage system."

"I've more than got the picture now."

"It dislodges bile."

"Now I'm beginning to feel a little nauseous, Mr Pollit, may we move on?"

"Nausea? It cures that too!"

"Mr Pollit, I have no wish to discuss the merits of Dr Crumpot's Remedy Syrup any longer."

"Even if I offered you ten fluid ounces for threepence? A special offer which is only available today."

"No thank you."

"And only available…" he raised a forefinger, "to ladies whose surname begins with C."

"No thank you, Mr Pollit."

"Ten fluid ounces is usually fourpence, Mrs Churchill. But as your surname begins with C then it's a mere thruppence."

"Why not P?" asked Pemberley.

"You might find that if you visit me again tomorrow then there is a special offer for surnames beginning with P," replied the pharmacist.

"Oh good, I'll be able to buy a bottle of Dr Crumpot's Remedy Syrup for threepence?"

"Perhaps even better, the letter P is quite close to my heart you see." He rested a hand on his chest to emphasise this and gave a wink.

"That is quite enough Mr Pollit," said Churchill. "We're not here to buy remedies, we're conducting a murder investigation. Now perhaps you can tell us when Gertie Pinks last visited to collect the Earl's medicine?"

He adopted a sullen expression. "I recall Gertie Pinks visiting just last week. A week earlier than usual."

"What do you mean by that?"

"She was dispatched once a month to collect the medicine and it was usually the third Thursday of every month. Well this Thursday is actually the third Thursday of this month but she came in last week to collect more telling me that the Earl of Middlemop was running low. I asked her to remind him that a little goes a long way and that he shouldn't be consuming too much. Overdosing on Dr Crumpot's Remedy Syrup can have drastic gastric effects."

"Golly. And you're quite sure that the maid arrived a week earlier than usual?"

"Yes, I usually dispensed eight bottles a month. But this past month, he appeared to have got through eight bottles in just three weeks."

"How interesting. Thank you Mr Pollit."

"Are you in need of a new loofah?"

"I can't believe you bought something from that man, Pembers," scorned Churchill once they were outside again.

"I don't like people who are constantly trying to sell me things."

"It's a present for Oswald," replied her assistant, handing the loofah to the dog. Oswald took it between his jaws and skipped off merrily down the high street.

"Wouldn't you say it's rather suspicious that Gertie fetched the Earl's monthly order of Dr Crumpot's Remedy Syrup a week early?" said Churchill as they sauntered after Oswald. "There can only be one reason for it and that's because someone wanted a bottle of the stuff which they could add the poison to!"

"You're not allowed to call it stuff, remember."

"I think we can call it what we like when Pollit the pharmacist is out of earshot, Pembers. It's probably nothing more than liquorice and rum anyway. All these supposed miracle cures are a waste of money as far as I'm concerned."

"But it brightens the eye."

"Poppycock."

"And straightens the back."

"Absolute hogwash."

"And eased the Earl's costive bowels, according to Tryphena."

"I really don't want to hear another word about the old man's tummy troubles. The reason he took the remedy syrup is irrelevant, the important matter is finding out when and how the cyanide was placed in the medicine bottle and who put it there."

"Pollit could have done it."

"He could have done, but why would he kill off a loyal customer?"

"It would be a silly thing to do. That's why parasites never kill their hosts."

"I don't warm to the pharmacist, Pembers, but I

wouldn't sink so low as to call him a parasite. We must acknowledge that he serves a purpose for people with mild ailments. Pembers... where have you gone?" Churchill glanced around frantically for her assistant who had seemingly vanished. Then she spied her cowering in the doorway of the grocer's. "What on earth are you doing?" she exclaimed, marching over to her. Pemberley ushered her away with a wave of her hand. "What on earth's the matter? Am I suddenly emitting an unpleasant odour?"

"No," hissed Pemberley. "I've just spied Mrs Higginbath heading towards us and I have an overdue library book."

"Oh golly."

"Pretend I'm not here!"

"Very well, I'll see her off, Pembers."

Churchill sauntered out into the middle of the high street whistling an improvised tune. The lumbering form of Mrs Higginbath was soon apparent, her stern, square face framed with long grey hair.

"Mrs Churchill," she announced.

"Oh good morning Mrs Higginbath, and how are you on this fine morning?"

"Is Miss Pemberley about?"

Churchill made a pretence of glancing around. "Not at the moment, I saw her not so long ago."

"How long ago?"

"Oh about... ten minutes ago. Maybe."

Mrs Higginbath peered past her. "Well she can't have gone far, I've just seen that dog of hers running about with what looks like a loofah in his mouth. Is he supposed to have that?"

"Yes I think so, but I shall go and check on him all the same." Churchill made a move to walk away.

"When you see Miss Pemberley, can you please inform her that she has an overdue library book."

"Of course."

"She's not usually late returning her books, I'm quite surprised at her."

"It must have slipped her mind, I'll remind her."

"*Notable Rock Formations in Shropshire* is the title. It was due back yesterday."

"Just one day overdue? I do admire the way you keep on top of things Mrs Higginbath."

The librarian gave a sniff. "I must say, Mrs Churchill, that you have my sympathy."

"Really? It's unlike you to feel any sympathy for me, Mrs Higginbath. May I ask why?"

"That business at the garden party. With the vicar and the petticoat."

"Are you referring to the failed elastic incident, Mrs Higginbath?"

"Yes. It must have been completely mortifying for you, you poor thing."

"But that wasn't me!"

"Well if it wasn't you, then who was it?"

"I don't know! But it certainly wasn't me. Who did you hear it from?"

"A number of people. I can understand why you'd wish to deny it, Mrs Churchill, it's not the sort of thing I would readily admit to either."

"I didn't!"

Mrs Higginbath gave a knowing nod. "Never mind, I'm sure everyone will forget about it soon enough. Remind Miss Pemberley about the book for me, won't you?"

Churchill felt a vice-like clench in her jaw as she watched Mrs Higginbath walk away.

Chapter 18

"TELL ME, PEMBERS," said Churchill, as she watched her kneeling assistant pick up pieces of shredded loofah from the office floor, "why the interest in rocks in Shropshire?"

"Oh I don't know really," Pemberley rested back on her heels. "I suppose I've always been rather fascinated by the Wenlock epoch."

"I can't imagine many people sharing your fascination with that. Except the author of the book you borrowed from the library."

"Lots of people are fascinated by it. Especially geologists."

"But you're not a geologist, Pembers."

"Why should it be only geologists who enjoy the Wenlock epoch? Other people should be allowed to as well."

"And no one's stopping you, Pembers. Even if they are rather baffled by it. I don't understand the connection with Shropshire."

"That's where the Wenlock rocks are. And the Wenlock

rocks gave their name to the second epoch of the Silurian period. Isn't that incredible?"

"If you say so."

"The Silurian is the third period of the Paleozoic era."

"Please don't tell me any more, Pembers. My brain is already filled with so much information that I'm worried that your trivia about rocks will push important things out of it."

"That won't happen, Mrs Churchill."

"It might! Just as I begin to understand the motivations of a particular suspect, I may find that the useful thoughts have suddenly been replaced with rocks and epochs. Now you should get that book returned to the library, I dread to think what Mrs Higginbath does to people who don't return their books on time."

"It's not pretty."

"I can imagine so. You're playing with fire there, Pembers."

"I like to live dangerously now and again." She got to her feet and dropped the pieces of loofah into the wastepaper basket.

"Clearly. Right, now we must prepare ourselves for the reading of the Earl of Middlemop's will at Gripedown Hall tomorrow. I have a feeling it might light a fire beneath the Ridley-Balls family."

"Really?"

"Of course! With rumours over the heir's parentage, how is the family going to feel when the inheritance goes to the basket weavers' son?"

"Did the Earl believe Humphrey was the basket weavers' son?"

"Now that's an interesting question, and one which we must ask people tomorrow."

"Because if he did, then he could have left his worldly goods to other family members instead."

"He could have. Do you know what I suspect, Pembers? I suspect that the Earl mentioned that he was going to make some changes in his will and the person who was set to be disinherited by those changes was the person who poisoned him."

"Before the changes could be made?"

"Exactly."

"So let's say, for example, that Humphrey knew he was set to inherit the Gripedown estate," said Pemberley, "then learned that the Earl was going to change his will because he believed the rumours about Humphrey being the basket weavers' son. That could mean that Humphrey murdered his grandfather before the change could be made?"

"Yes indeed."

"So Humphrey is our prime suspect!"

"That all depends on what the will says tomorrow."

"So the person named in the will is the culprit? They have to be, in fact, don't they? If the Earl was murdered before he could change his will, then the beneficiary of the most recent version of his will is the murderer!"

"It's a good theory."

"And we'll find out tomorrow! The case will be solved, Mrs Churchill!"

"It could. Although part of me doubts if it will be that simple."

Chapter 19

LARGE-EARED ARISTOCRATS STARED out of dingy oil paintings at their descendants gathering in the drawing room of Gripedown Hall the following morning. A well-polished table was set at one end of the room and rows of chairs were arranged neatly before it. The tall windows on one side of the room afforded a view of the fountain with its tiers of lions and cherubs.

Churchill and Pemberley took their places in good time so they could observe everyone else as they arrived.

"They need Mrs Bouton to freshen this place up," murmured Churchill as she surveyed the faded furnishings. "The wallpaper looks older than us, Pembers." She gave Tryphena a cheerful wave as her friend entered the room, then she acknowledged Inspector Mappin with a polite nod.

"Now who's this, could it be Cairistiona Vigors-Slip-cote?" she whispered.

The woman who had just entered the room was wide-faced, like Tryphena, and her ears peeked out through her grey, bobbed hair. Her eyes were languid and she wore a dress of insipid colour which hung from her shoulders like laundry left out to dry.

"It must be Tryphena's sister," whispered Pemberley in reply. "Although she doesn't seem quite as perky."

"Well I suppose her father has just been murdered, so we should consider that in our assessment of her appearance."

The family solicitor, Mr Verney, marched officiously into the room and headed for the polished table. He was short, bespectacled, and wore an expensive-looking pinstriped suit. A young man, weighed down by folders and papers, followed closely behind him.

As the solicitor made himself comfortable at the table, Churchill observed a smartly-dressed man, about forty years old, sidle in through the door.

"Do you think that's Humphrey?" she whispered to Pemberley. "The ninth Earl of Middlemop?"

"It must be."

Churchill had always imagined a changeling to be unpleasant in appearance, but this man was quite the opposite. His looks were handsome with dark hair, dark whiskers and hazel coloured eyes. Most noticeable of all were his ears which were normally sized, quite unlike those of his family members.

Was it possible that he was the son of the basket weavers? Churchill now considered there could be some truth in it. Why else would the grandson bear so little resemblance to those around him?

The final person to arrive was Aunt Nora in her bath chair. Her face was just visible beneath the wide brim of her straw hat.

"Poor old lady, Pembers, I expect the past half hour has just been spent carrying her down all those stairs. How impractical."

Mr Verney cleared his throat and fixed his eyes on a bundle of papers on the table in front of him.

"I shall now read out the will of Richard Aubrey Ridley-Balls, the eighth Earl of Middlemop, of Gripedown Hall, Compton Poppleford," he announced. Everyone listened in hushed silence.

"'I, Richard Aubrey Ridley-Balls, the eighth Earl of Middlemop, of Gripedown Hall, Compton Poppleford, in the county of Dorset, hereby declare this to be my last will and testament, revoking all wills and codicils made heretofore by me,'" said the solicitor in a dry, dull voice.

"'I give to my daughter, Cairistiona Vigors-Slipcote, my library of books and prints.'"

"Books?" The languid-faced woman gave a sniff and glanced around as if expecting everyone to share her disappointment.

"'I give to my daughter, Tryphena Ridley-Balls, my watch, shirt studs and shirt pins.'"

"Pins?" Tryphena pushed her mouth and nose together into a puzzled snout.

"'I give to each of my granddaughters the sum of one thousand pounds.'" This appeared to please some of the younger ladies in the room.

"Goodness. Humphrey must be getting the rest, no wonder the rest of the family doesn't like him," whispered Churchill.

"Who's getting the house?" called out a voice from the back of the room.

Mr Verney cleared his throat and scanned his eyes over the people in front of him before slowly returning them to the paper he'd been reading from. His nose gave a satisfactory twitch as if he were enjoying this moment of authority and suspense.

"'I devise and bequeath all my real estate, in its entirety…'"

Eyes rested on Humphrey Ridley-Balls whose expression remained impassive.

"'To my faithful old housekeeper Mrs Susannah Surpant,'" added Mr Verney.

The silence was replaced by an even deeper quiet. Everyone glanced around at each other, searching for the face of the lucky beneficiary.

"What?" snapped Cairistiona. "The *housekeeper*?"

Mrs Surpant stood at the back of the room with her arms folded and one side of her thin mouth raised a little.

"Mr Verney," said Tryphena, marching over to the table. "I'd like to have a closer look at this if I may."

"And so would I!" fumed Cairistiona, joining her. "Do I really only get *books*?"

"Yes you do, Cairistiona," responded Tryphena. "At least I get Daddy's watch."

"Where's that housekeeper?" snarled her sister.

"Here," said a calm Mrs Surpant, stepping forward. The faint smile remained as she regarded everyone else with a superior gaze.

"What about the ninth Earl of Middlemop?" called out Churchill. "Does he get anything more than a title?" She looked around for the handsome young man but he appeared to have left the room.

Tryphena shook her head dismissively. "No, Annabel," she replied. "At least Daddy saw sense about him."

"I'd rather he got the house than that Surpant woman!" fumed Cairistiona. "She's a servant! Since when did a servant inherit the estate of a four-hundred-year-old peerage? Show me Father's signature on the will please, Mr Verney."

The solicitor passed the papers over to her with a sigh.

She peered closely at the will, then put her spectacles on and examined it even more closely. "Is this his signature, Tryphena?"

"It looks like it."

"I know it looks like it! It's hardly not going to look like it, is it? But *is it* his signature?"

"Well it has to be, presumably he signed it in the presence of the two witnesses named here."

"Gertie Pinks and Robert Humphries," announced Cairistiona. "A maid and the chauffeur. They must be in on this too!"

"Can someone fetch Miss Pinks and Mr Humphries, please?" asked Mr Verney.

Everyone in the room began muttering as they waited for the two servants to arrive.

"Golly, Pembers, this is an entertaining spectacle, isn't it?" said Churchill. "We should have brought some provisions to help us enjoy the show. In fact, I must confess that I have an emergency eclair in my handbag. Do you think it would be rude to partake?"

"You can't eat eclairs at the reading of a will, Mrs Churchill."

"I can't imagine anyone's ever made it a rule."

"It would be covered under general etiquette."

"I suppose it would."

"But at least we have our main suspect now," whispered Pemberley.

"You think it's Mrs Surpant?"

"Of course! Wasn't that what we discussed yesterday? Whoever's named in the will is the person who bumped him off. She must have persuaded him to leave everything to her and then he must have intimated that he was going to change it and she struck before he could do so."

"She certainly had access to his remedy syrup, all we'd

need to do is establish where she obtained the cyanide from."

"That's easy enough, perhaps it's used to fumigate the conservatory or maybe she knows a photographer? They use it as a fixing agent."

"Since when did you know about photography, Pembers?"

"The lady of international travel befriended one in Paris. I was his muse for a short while."

"A photographer's muse, Pembers? Crikey. Do you have any of the photographs from those days?"

"No I destroyed them."

"Gosh. Anyway, it seems that it would be rather straightforward for Mrs Surpant to poison the Earl. She was free to enter his bathroom without rousing suspicion and it now appears that she had a motive. But I wonder, Pembers, isn't it *too* obvious that it's her?"

Heads turned as the maid and chauffeur entered the room and joined Mr Verney at the table.

"Miss Pinks, please confirm that you witnessed the eighth Earl of Middlemop sign his will," said the solicitor. "You saw him sign it here, am I right? Six weeks ago on the tenth of May?"

"Yeah that's right," said Gertie. "I remember like it was yesterday. He was sat in 'is office and he called me in and told me I needed to witness him signing somethin', then he told me to go fetch someone else. Anyone he said. I'd just been out feedin' the pigs and I'd seen Mr Humphries shinin' up the car so I thought I'd go and fetch 'im."

"Mr Humphries, you signed this document with Miss Pinks and your employer?" asked the solicitor.

"That is correct sir. It was mid-morning as I recall. I was buffing up the Daimler when Miss Pinks here summoned me."

"Well there we have it," said Mr Verney, addressing the two sisters. "Both witnesses confirm that they witnessed your father, the Earl of Middlemop, sign this document. There is no reason to question the fact this is his signature and the contents of his last will and testament therefore stand as they are." He and his assistant began to pack away the papers.

"Ridiculous!" raged Cairistiona. "An absolute scandal!"

"It's a farce!" seethed Tryphena. "Daddy must have lost his mind! It makes no sense. You got your claws into him, Mrs Surpant, that's for sure. What can a mere house-keeper possibly want with Gripedown Hall?"

Spots of colour appeared in Mrs Surpant's pale face. "He knew that not one of you would look after the estate properly. That's why he left it to me!" she retorted. "I know how to run it whereas you just lounged around in your estate cottage never lifting a finger. Why should he leave it to you and your lazy sister? With his son deceased, there was no one else sensible to inherit it."

"Do you know what I think, Mrs Surpant?" The steel waves of Tryphena's hair trembled angrily. "I think that you cajoled him into naming you in his will! You pressured, coerced, bullied and intimidated poor Daddy into making you his beneficiary. And do you know what I also think? I think you were terribly worried that he would come to his senses and change his will back to how it was before and that you would be left out of it. And to make sure that you inherited the estate, you poisoned him before he could change it again!"

Mrs Surpant's jaw fell open. "Are you accusing me of *murder*, Miss Ridley-Balls?"

"Yes I am!"

Chapter 20

"Me? A murderer? I've never heard anything more ridiculous in all my days!" exclaimed Mrs Surpant.

"Well I've heard something that's more ridiculous," retorted Tryphena. "And that's you being named as the beneficiary in Daddy's will!"

"I will not stand here and have you screeching at me like an alley cat," replied the housekeeper. "Especially in my own home."

And with those words, she turned heel and left the room.

"*My own home?*" echoed Tryphena, her mouth hanging open as she stared at her sister. "Can you believe it Carrie?"

"No, there has to be some mistake."

Churchill noticed Mr Verney and his assistant quietly leave, heads bowed as if trying to escape the sisters' notice.

"Inspector Mappin!" called out Tryphena. "I order you to arrest Mrs Surpant!"

"Well I don't know about that," responded the brown-whiskered inspector. "I need a little more—"

"A little more *what*?"

"Evidence, for one thing."

"But isn't it obvious?"

"It seems obvious, but…"

"Come along, Pembers," whispered Churchill, let's leave Mappin and Tryph to it, there isn't much more we can do here."

The two ladies made their escape and began walking along the corridor to the entrance hall.

"It seems our work is done," said Pemberley. "Tryphena's solved the case."

"But has she?"

"Who else could it be?"

"There's Mr Goldbeam for one."

"But he only unblocked the chimney."

"That's what he claims he did. And there's Mr Porge. Where's he got to? He seems to be keeping a low profile."

Churchill turned as she heard footsteps and a trundling sound behind her.

"Good morning Mrs Ponsonby-Staithes!" she said to the old lady in her bath chair. "Quite a surprising outcome this morning, wouldn't you say?"

"Nothing surprises me any more about this family," replied Aunt Nora with a dismissive wave of her hand.

"I see." The nurse pushed Aunt Nora past them to the entrance hall where two footmen waited at the foot of the staircase.

"Gertie!" said Churchill cheerily as the maid now appeared. "What do you think about Mrs Surpant and the will?"

"Strange, ain't it?" replied the maid. "And ter think this place belongs ter the 'ousekeeper now! Don't seem right, do it?"

"It's going to take some people a while to grow accustomed to."

"Tell yer what I don't understand, and that's what 'appened ter the other one."

"Other what?"

"Will."

"Another will?"

"Yeah, 'is lordship asked me ter sign another one."

"When?"

"After I signed the one wiv Mr Humphries."

"So there's a more recent will?"

"Fink so."

"Who was the other witness?"

"Mr Porge."

"You and Mr Porge witnessed the Earl signing a different will to the one which Mr Verney just read out?"

"Yeah."

"Are you sure about this, Gertie?"

"Yeah."

"How sure?"

"A lot sure."

"Goodness. Surely Mr Verney must know something about this? But he's just left. Actually, we may be able to catch him."

She darted off into the entrance hall.

"Do yer want me to come too?" Gertie called after her.

"Yes! Quick!"

The two ladies and the maid dashed through the hall to the main door, they had just reached the top of the steps as a shiny car began to pull away on the driveway. Churchill could make out the bespectacled face of Mr Verney behind the wheel.

"Wait!" She cried out with a wave of her arms. She scrambled down the steps, trying not to twist her ankle.

"Wait!" she called out again to the car. Pemberley did the same. The car began to slow then came to an abrupt halt. Mr Verney wound down the window as Churchill puffed her way up to him.

"What is it?" he snapped. "Don't tell me someone else has been murdered over the inheritance now."

"Th-th there's another one," panted Churchill. "Another will."

"Another will?" replied the solicitor. "What are you talking about?"

"Gertie. Miss Pinks. Here she is." Pemberley and the maid were now at Churchill's side. "She signed another one, tell him Gertie."

The maid repeated to the solicitor what she had just told Churchill in the corridor.

"It's irrelevant," he replied. "The will I read out this morning supersedes all previous wills. It states, 'I hereby declare this to be my last will and testament, revoking all wills and codicils made heretofore by me.'"

"Miss Pink maintains that the will she signed with Mr Porge was *after* the will she signed with Mr Humphries."

"It can't have been a will."

"So what could it have been?"

"I don't know, but I've only drafted one will with the Earl in the past year."

"Perhaps he used another law firm?"

"Another law firm? My firm has provided its services to the Earl of Middlemop and his family for over forty years!"

"Exclusively?"

The solicitor opened and closed his mouth like a gold-fish. "I would have thought so," he said eventually.

"But you can't be sure?"

"At this very moment, Mrs Churchill, I don't think anyone can be particularly sure about anything."

"When the Earl drafted his will with you, did he explain the reasoning behind his choices?"

"What passed between my client and I was a confidential conversation. Now, if you'll excuse me, I have another appointment to get to."

The window wound up and the car pulled away.

"So he doesn't believe us!" protested Churchill with a stamp of her foot. "Gertie, Miss Pemberley, let's go and find Mr Porge!"

"I recall signing a will a few weeks ago," said Mr Porge. After some searching, they'd found him in the wine cellar examining some dusty bottles.

"Can you recall exactly when?" asked Churchill.

"It would have been around the end of May."

"And Miss Pinks here says she was also present. Do you recall her being there?"

His eyes rested on the young maid. "Yes, Miss Pinks was also there."

"The will which the family solicitor read out this morning was dated the tenth of May, however it seems that you and Miss Pinks signed another will which was dated after that."

"How intriguing."

"It certainly is. Did the Earl ever discuss the contents of his will with you, Mr Porge?"

"Absolutely not, his will was his own private matter."

"Well, the long and the short of it is that Mrs Surpant has been named as the inheritor of the Gripedown Estate this morning but, in fact, it may be someone else entirely. Have you any idea where the will you witnessed could be now?"

"It would be among his private papers, I haven't yet sorted through them all yet."

"Would you like to sort through them now so we can find the other will?"

"Not now, Mrs Churchill, I'm taking an inventory of the wine."

She felt a snap of impatience. "Can't the wine wait?"

"It's a quarterly task which I carry out on the third Tuesday of every third month."

"While I admire your dedication to the Earl's wines, Mr Porge, I would urge you please to help us look for the will which you witnessed. It's a matter of urgency and may well resolve the rather heated arguments which are occurring upstairs at this moment."

The butler gave a sigh. "Very well."

"We can all give you a hand if it's a lot of work, Mr Porge."

"There is no need, it's not a lot of work."

"Jolly good. So you're going to look through his papers now?"

He replaced the bottle next to its equally dusty counterparts. "If I must."

"Thank you so much, Mr Porge. We'll hang about and see what you manage to find."

Chapter 21

"Right then, time to find Tryphena and Cairistiona and tell them about the second will," said Churchill to Pemberley and Gertie as they marched back to the drawing room.

"And Mrs Surpant," added Pemberley. "She's not going to take too kindly to the news."

"It all depends if she's the main beneficiary of the second will, doesn't it? You're right though, the element of doubt which the second will introduces won't be pleasant for her."

Gertie gave a snigger.

"Are you all right there?"

"Mrs Surpant's going to be very annoyed."

They encountered Tryphena outside the library. "Oh there you are Gertie," she said. "Where have you been? Mrs Vigors-Slipcote and I need lots of coffee."

"Gertie will fetch it in a moment, Tryph," said Churchill. "But first of all, let me tell you where she's been. Young Gertie here has been helping us with our investigation and we have established that your father made a new will after the one which Mr Verney read out today."

Tryphena's eyes grew wide. "Another will? What does it say?"

"We don't know."

"So how do you know about it?"

"Your father asked Gertie and Mr Porge to witness his signature on it. It was at the end of May, apparently, dated after the will which Mr Verney had in his hot little hands this morning."

"Golly! Where is it then?"

Mr Porge has gone to look through your father's papers.

"I'll go and help him!" Tryphena took off before Churchill could say another word.

"Looks like the coffee isn't quite so urgent after all, Gertie," said Churchill. She noticed a tall, dark form gliding towards them. "However, Mrs Surpant will no doubt have a chore for you instead."

The housekeeper reached them. "The linen needs folding, Gertie," she snapped at the maid.

"Just before Gertie goes off to do that, I would like to speak to you both about Dr Crumpot's Remedy Syrup," said Churchill.

"As long as it's quick," responded the housekeeper tartly.

"Miss Pemberley and I spoke with Mr Pollit the pharmacist who was the supplier of the remedy syrup, is that right?"

The housekeeper gave a nod.

"He told us that young Gertie here collected the supply once a month and that the last collection was made a week earlier than usual."

"Well I don't think that was unusual."

"Had it been collected a week early before?"

"I'm sure it would have been."

"What do you say, Gertie?"

"I don't recall." The maid bit her lip and gave Mrs Surpant a sideways glance.

"Mr Pollit told us that the bottles were always collected on the third Thursday of every month."

"Well Mr Pollit is clearly a stickler for these things," replied the housekeeper. "I can't say that I noticed the collection date falling with such regularity."

"Are you really sure about that?"

"Of course I am, Mrs Churchill, and I consider it rather impudent of you to question my word."

"Gertie, may I ask why you collected the bottles when you did?"

"Mrs Surpant told me to."

"I see."

"Only because Gertie told me that supplies were running low," responded the housekeeper.

"Right." Churchill glanced from one to the other, interested in how neither wished to claim responsibility. "But were you not concerned, Mrs Surpant, that for the supplies to run low, the Earl was consuming more than he should have?"

"Not concerned at all, no. And whether the bottles were picked up a week earlier than usual or not, I don't see why the fact has any bearing on the Earl's poisoning."

"Well someone could have been planning subterfuge you see, perhaps they wanted some extra bottles to tamper with?"

"And by that someone, you're suggesting myself or Gertie?"

"No, not at all. I was interested, in fact, to find out if someone had asked you to collect those bottles early."

"No they didn't. And I've had enough accusations of murder being thrown at me today thank you, Mrs Churchill. I'm becoming rather tired of having to defend myself."

"I wish to make it clear that I wasn't accusing you of anything, Mrs Surpant, I merely wished to clear the matter up. Anything anomalous or out of the ordinary should be checked you see. It's the detective's way. And, while we're at it, there's another matter I'd like to clear up. Mr Goldbeam told us that when he unblocked the chimney in the Earl's room, he pulled out some papers. However, I recall you telling us it was a bird's nest."

"Did I?"

"Yes. So I'm wondering why you told us the blockage was a bird's nest when Mr Goldbeam told us it was a bundle of papers."

The housekeeper's face tightened. "I must have confused this particular blockage with another one. I certainly recall Mr Goldbeam retrieving a bird's nest from the Earl's chimney, that must have been on a previous occasion."

"Mr Goldbeam said that he put the papers on the Earl's writing desk, did you see them there?"

"I can't say I did, no."

"Perhaps Mr Porge tidied them away?"

"Perhaps he did. I advise that you check with him."

"Was the Earl in the habit of pushing papers up his chimney?"

"No, I'd not known him to do it before."

"Do you think someone else could have done it?"

"Such as who?"

"I've no idea, Mrs Surpant, that's why I asked."

"I can't think who else would have done it. Now you really must excuse me, Gertie and I must be getting on."

"Of course. All hands on deck are probably needed now to find this mysterious second will."

The housekeeper's jaw dropped. "Second will? What are you talking about?"

"You've not heard yet? It seems your employer made a second will and we need to find it."

The housekeeper took a small step back as if trying to accommodate a punch to the stomach.

"I see." She pursed her lips. "Let's leave the laundry until later then, Gertie, and have a look for it."

Churchill and Pemberley watched the two servants depart.

"Now do you suppose she already knew about the second will, Pembers?"

"It's difficult to say."

"It certainly is. Perhaps it was among the papers which were shoved up the chimney. Whoever hid them there can't have expected them to stay there, could they? Either the draw of the fire would be interfered with or the papers would be damaged. Burnt even. They must have been put there hurriedly, perhaps hidden when someone was heard to approach the room, and the person who hid them there intended to retrieve them a short while later."

"Mrs Surpant was quite dismissive about the remedy syrup being collected sooner than usual."

"She was, wasn't she? I feel quite certain she's trying to cover something up. Now there are a few more people we need to speak to, Pembers, Cairistiona being one of them. Let's pounce on her before she gets caught up in the search for the will too."

Chapter 22

AFTER A BRIEF SEARCH, Churchill and Pemberley found Cairistiona in a window seat in the morning room.

"Oh, I was hoping you were the maid bringing in the coffee."

"I think she's been sent off to fold linen now."

"What does one have to do to get a coffee in this place?"

"One might have to resort to making it oneself."

She laughed, seemingly finding the thought inordinately funny. "You're the two detective ladies aren't you? Tryphena told me all about you. Mind if I smoke?"

"Not at all."

"Aren't you the lady whose skirt fell down at the garden party?" she asked, once her cigarette was lit.

"No, that wasn't me."

"I felt sure I remember the name Churchill being mentioned."

"Perhaps it was, but it certainly wasn't my skirt which slipped down. Now then, the outcome of your father's will has been quite a surprise hasn't it?"

"You can say that again." She blew out a plume of smoke. "I thought the lot would go to Humphrey. I had no idea Papa would consider leaving it all to Surpant."

"Were you hoping for a little more yourself?"

"Of course! Books and prints. After everything I did for that man? Clearly the housekeeper wormed her way into his affections. I can imagine her squirming like a worm, can't you Mrs Churchill?"

"I can't say I've given the image much thought."

"She will have seduced him of course."

"Cripes, do you think so?"

Pemberley tried to suppress a gagging noise.

"Why else would he leave her everything?" continued Cairistiona. "She crept insidiously into his life like a slow release of poisonous gas."

"Gosh. Do you think she's responsible for his death?"

"Yes! I think it's quite obvious now that old Surpant poisoned poor dear Papa. And the police inspector wants more evidence! Can you believe it?"

"Well that's Inspector Mappin for you."

"I've a good mind to get Scotland Yard down here, they'll soon have her charged. There's absolutely no chance of this place falling into her hands, that's for sure. How foolish does she think we all are?"

"You live some distance away, is that right?"

"Hoffmanner Manor. It's the other side of Harneth Cublet."

"Wherever that may be."

"East of here, near Fidgeworth Dendelbury."

Churchill glanced at the notebook in Pemberley's hand and gave her a nod to write this down.

"You live some distance away, and yet—"

"Well I wouldn't describe it as some distance, it's quite near actually!" she interrupted with a laugh.

"I see. Well, it's not exactly down the road is it?"

"No. What of it?"

"And yet your sister tells me that you've been a regular visitor to Gripedown Hall of late."

"It's my home!"

"It was your home as a child, Hoffmanner Manor is your home. You share it with your husband Mr Vigors-Slipcote, am I right?"

"Yes, to be honest with you, that's why I'm often here. It's because he's always there."

"I see. Your marriage is unhappy?"

"No it's perfectly happy! As long as we spend as little time as possible together then we're both as merry as larks."

"I'm pleased to hear it. You do, however, appear to have spent an increasing amount of time at Gripedown in recent weeks from what your sister tells me."

"Well I don't know what Tryphena is getting at when she mentions that to you but I concede that there is some truth in it and it's because I wanted to spend as much time as possible with dear Papa. He was ninety-nine years of age and I knew he wouldn't have long left."

"I didn't know your dear papa, Mrs Vigors-Slipcote, however I have heard that he was rather an unsociable type. Did he appreciate you spending quite so much time with him?"

"Oh he was completely unsociable! And it was nothing to do with his age either, he was always unsociable. People were apt to blame his shortcomings on his age and I was quick to correct them, he had always been like that!"

"And yet you wished to spend as much time as possible with him during his final weeks? Not that you knew they were to be his final weeks, of course, he could have lived on a few years longer."

"He wasn't going to, he was close to the end." Cairistiona gave a sorrowful sniff.

"How did you know?"

"I just had an inkling. I knew that each moment I spent with him would be precious."

"And how did you spend these precious last few weeks with him?"

"We played cards and went for walks. I read to him an awful lot, we got through most of Dickens."

"In just a few weeks?" queried Pemberley. "You must have been reading to him practically non-stop."

Cairistiona scowled. "We did the popular stories, not the more obscure ones like David whatever-it-is."

"*David Copperfield?*" responded Pemberley. "That's one of his best."

"Oh well, we didn't get to do that one. The one with the old lady in the wedding dress, which one's that one again?"

Churchill glanced at Pemberley, hoping she'd have the answer.

"*Great Expectations*," replied her reliable assistant.

"That's the one," said Cairistiona. "We read a bit of that."

"So when you say you got through most of Dickens, you actually only read him a chapter or two of *Great Expectations*," said Churchill.

"Yes I suppose I did really. Believe me it felt like most of Dickens at the time." She glowered at Pemberley as if irritated that she'd queried her story.

"And when did you last see your father?" Churchill asked.

Cairistiona's lower lip began to tremble. "Oh!" she gasped as she smothered her mouth and nose with her handkerchief. Churchill gave Pemberley a sceptical glance while the two ladies allowed her to recover from her show of emotion.

"It was… it was… ab-ab about four o'clock that day," replied Cairistiona eventually, her bosom heaving with upset. "I saw… I saw… him outside by the fountain with Try-Try Tryphena. They appeared to be having the most terrible bust-up about something and she looked awfully angry."

"A bust up? Do you know what it was about?"

"I couldn't tell you, I'm afraid. I have absolutely no idea. You'll have to ask Tryphena about it."

"That was the last time you saw your father?"

"Yes! When Tryphena was shouting at him!" She emitted a loud sob.

"Did you not go and see your father after the incident to find out if he was all right?"

Cairistiona held her breath for a moment, as if considering that this might have been a good idea. "I wanted to…" she began, then paused to suck on her cigarette. "But I was waylaid by someone. Mrs Surpant I think it was. She waylaid me."

"Where were you when you witnessed your father and sister having the argument?"

"In the drawing room. I was looking at them through the window."

"And then you were waylaid. By someone coming into the room?"

"Yes, that's exactly what happened and I feel quite sure that it was erm… actually it wasn't Mrs Surpant, it was Mr Porge asking about some small matter. He can verify that of course, you only need ask him."

"I see. What was the small matter?"

"Oh, some household matter, I recall it was quite important at the time however such things pale into insignificance as soon as someone's murdered don't they? And now I can't, for the life of me, recall what it was all about."

"Mr Porge will remember, presumably? He seems a man who remains unflustered."

"Nothing seems to fluster him at all. He may well remember but then again he may not."

"Well thank you Mrs Vigors-Slipcote, this conversation has been immensely helpful."

"Has it? I don't see how."

"Well it has. We'll leave you be now, you'll probably want to help the others look for the second will."

She stared at them, face agog.

"Second will? What *second will?*"

Chapter 23

"Now come along, Oswald, it's time to go," called Churchill to the little dog who was chasing Margery around the fountain.

"He doesn't want to leave his friend," said Pemberley.

"I realise that but Mr Speakman is waiting in his taxi."

"Why don't we take Margery with us?"

"Because she's not our dog, she belongs to the Ridley-Balls."

"Poor Margery."

"Now please go and fetch your dog, Pembers, Mr Speakman's meter will be running. I've never known a taxi meter tick over as fast as his."

Margery watched forlornly from the driveway as the taxi pulled away.

"I can't believe we're just leaving her behind," lamented Pemberley.

"At her home," replied Churchill. "I can't see the problem in that."

"She misses Oswald when he's away."

"I'm sure she does. But we'll be back again before we

know it. Thank goodness Tryphena is reimbursing our taxi fares. Now then, did you think Cairistiona was a little cagey just now?"

"She was vague about some things and unnecessarily comprehensive about others."

"Exactly what I think. I'm so glad we work together, we share some common thought processes don't we?"

"Some."

"There's something not right about her at all. But I don't see what motive she'd have for poisoning her father, especially when the housekeeper ended up with all the spoils."

"But there's the second will though, maybe she was counting on that?"

"I don't think she knew of it, you saw her reaction when we told her. Perhaps she's a good actress but her surprised response seemed genuine to me."

"I don't think there's anything genuine about anyone in that house. And interesting to hear more about Tryphena's argument with the Earl, don't you think?"

"But dear old Tryph can't possibly have had anything to do with his poisoning!"

"So why hasn't she told you yet about the argument by the fountain?"

Churchill felt a pang of resentment that her friend might be hiding something from her, but she felt the need to defend her in case it was an honest mistake. "It must have slipped her mind. She's had a terrible upset, the poor thing."

"We can't rule her out Mrs Churchill. I think both sisters are a little bit shifty if you ask me. It's awful to hear myself say it but I don't think that Cairistiona's tears for her poor departed father were genuine."

"They seemed a little over-egged. Then again people do grieve in different ways."

"You're right there, perhaps we should be careful not to judge her too harshly. Mind you, it's rather difficult isn't it? What an annoying snivelling face she had at times."

"I think it's odd that Cairistiona didn't enquire after her father's welfare after witnessing the argument," said Churchill. "I think she would have gone to see him to ensure that he wasn't too upset by it. In fact she could even have intervened at the time, I wonder why she didn't?"

"That could mean one of two things: either the argument didn't happen or she didn't care about her father as much as she claimed."

"She was waylaid by Mr Porge was her vague explanation. We'll need to verify that with the butler. There's rather a lot that doesn't add up. And now I expect they're all very busy looking for that second will. Most odd though, don't you think, Pembers? I wonder why the Earl chose to make a second will without informing Mr Verney."

"Maybe he fell out with Mr Verney."

"Perhaps he did. So why didn't Mr Verney tell us that? On second thought, I don't suppose he would do, would he? So the Earl could have fallen out with him and used another solicitor to draw up the second will. How many law firms are there in Compton Poppleford?"

"I have no idea."

"Well there must be a few, mustn't there? Perhaps five?"

"I don't know."

"Well it's not going to be thirty or anything as much as that. It can only be a handful. If push comes to shove, we'll need to work our way round them asking if they drafted a will for the Earl."

～

After stopping off at the bakery, the two ladies returned to their office.

"What a morning, Pembers. You put on the kettle and I'll lay out the jam and cream fingers. Then we can have a nice sit down and—"

Churchill was interrupted by the sound of footsteps on the stairs.

"Oh what now? Do you know what, Pembers? I expect that's Mrs Th—"

Their red-haired friend marched into the room.

"Oh there you are!" she flustered. "I tried calling round earlier and there was no sign of you."

"That's because we were on an important investigation, Mrs Thonnings."

She gave a sigh and sank down into the chair opposite Churchill. "Oh, jam and cream fingers!" Her eyes lit up.

"Yes and we haven't had any ourselves yet."

"Well there are enough there for… about six people I should say."

"We're rather peckish, Mrs Thonnings. There was no opportunity to stop for elevenses this morning. Now what can we help you with?"

"Isn't it obvious?"

"Not immediately no. However, I am aware that you've asked us to look into Mrs Bouton and the malicious letters in the *Compton Poppleford Gazette*. Could it be something to do with that?"

"Of course it is. Have you got any further with it yet?"

"Not since we last saw you I'm afraid, Mrs Thonnings. We've been involved in an important murder investigation as you know."

Mrs Thonnings gave a sigh and looked down at her hands in her lap.

"Yes I realise that," she said in a small voice. "I just thought that maybe… oh, it doesn't matter. I realise you're so busy Mrs Churchill and perhaps it was a mistake of mine to think that…. Never mind. I only had one customer yesterday and all she bought were six buttons and a yard of lace. I suppose if this goes on for much longer then I'll have to think about closing my doors, I never thought it would come to this but—"

"Now, now, Mrs Thonnings," interrupted Churchill. The haberdasher's attempt to make her feel guilty was having the desired effect. "We do have time to work on the case, in fact I'm already feeling rather bored by wills and remedy syrup. It was rather pressing that we were at Gripedown Hall this morning but I should think we'll be able to find a little time this afternoon to work on your case. Wouldn't you say, Miss Pemberley?" Her assistant placed the tea tray on her desk.

"Yes. I'm rather bored of wills and remedy syrup too. I think the whole silly crowd have only got themselves to blame."

"That's taking it a little too far, Miss Pemberley. Let's not forget that a defenceless old man had his life tragically cut short by the act of a selfish and cruel individual. If we don't find out who it is then they could do the same to someone else."

"Well we know who it is."

"Who?" asked Mrs Thonnings.

"Mrs Surpant," replied Pemberley.

"That miserable old crow?" responded Mrs Thonnings. "I can't say I ever warmed to her, but I can't believe she murdered the Earl!"

"We can't be sure yet," interjected Churchill. "I fear that Miss Pemberley is jumping the gun a little."

"Well you said it yourself too, Mrs Churchill."

"She's certainly a suspect. But there's a lot more work to do yet. Anyway, Mrs Thonnings, we shall work on the case of the poison elastic letters this afternoon."

"Don't you mean poison pen letters?"

"Well I do, but I thought poison elastic sounds quite good, wouldn't you say?"

"I certainly wouldn't want a skirt made with that," said Pemberley.

"I've been trying to spruce up the shop a little," said Mrs Thonnings.

"Well that's a good start."

"I swallowed my pride and asked Mr Goldbeam if he could give the shopfront a lick of paint."

"That's excellent and much needed. I think a repaint will work wonders. Have you decided on a colour?"

"A pretty shade of blue."

"Wonderful, it will look delightful."

"Except Mr Goldbeam is refusing to do it. I've even offered to pay him."

"Refusing? Why?"

"I suppose I didn't realise how upset he was by my decision to move on to a new man friend."

"Oh dear, so it's something to do with that. You've swallowed your pride but he hasn't swallowed his?"

"Yes I'm afraid that's the situation. So there's only so much sprucing up I can do."

"Surely there must be someone else who can help? Mr Goldbeam can't be the only person in the village who's any good at painting shopfronts."

"Well he is the best."

"Then you'll just have to settle for second best. Now

then, while we've been sitting here chatting, I've thought of a plan."

"Really? You can think and chat at the same time, Mrs Churchill?"

"Absolutely. It's how a detective's mind works. Miss Pemberley and I will visit the reporter Smithy Miggins and ask to see the poison elastic letters."

"And what if he won't show us?" asked Pemberley.

"That's a distinct possibility but there's no harm in asking."

"He'll just say no," said Mrs Thonnings. "I know it."

"Hold on a moment, there's a jam and cream finger missing," declared Churchill. "I'm sure I put six on the plate and now there are only five! Did you take one, Mrs Thonnings?"

The haberdasher checked her watch. "Goodness, look at the time. I'd better get back to my shop."

Chapter 24

"The thing is, a reporter never reveals his sources," said Smithy Miggins, exhaling a ring of smoke. His jacket was as greasy as his lank hair and his eyes were shifty. He stood with Churchill and Pemberley in the yard behind the *Compton Poppleford Gazette* offices. "Is that your dog?" He pointed his limp, rolled-up cigarette at Oswald who was involved in a staring competition with a cat perched on a water butt.

"Yes he is," responded Churchill. "And we're not asking you to reveal your sources, Mr Miggins. Besides, how can you possibly know them? You reported that the letters were anonymous."

"They are."

"So even you don't know who your sources are."

"Your dog needs to watch that cat. She'll attack him bad if he gets anywhere near her. She tried to scratch my eyes out once."

"What on earth were you trying to do to her?"

"Nothing! I was just walking past. A beast she is."

"May we see the anonymous letters you were sent, Mr Miggins?"

"I don't reveal my sources, I told you!"

"You're not revealing them. And anyway, if Miss Pemberley and I recognise the handwriting then you'll actually find out who your sources are. We could be quite useful to you, have you considered that?"

"You'd recognise the handwriting, would you?"

"Possibly. But how do we know until we actually see them?"

He gave this some thought as he gave another puff on his cigarette.

"They chose to be anonymous for a reason," he said eventually. "So there's no way that I'm letting you have a look at those letters. If you recognise the handwriting then you'll know whose socks were crumpled and whose drawers almost slipped down. Come to think of it…" He pointed his cigarette in Churchill's direction. "I heard a rumour that it was your skirt that fell down at the garden party, Mrs Churchill!"

"It was not me! It's a false rumour I tell you." She felt a flush of shame as he gave a laugh.

"You've come here to get your letter back, is that it?"

"It was not me at the garden party, Mr Miggins, let me make that clear!" Then she thought again about what he'd just said. She took a calming breath before speaking again. "Are you suggesting that if the people who wrote those letters ask for them back, then you'll return them?"

He gave a shrug. "Only if they admitted they wrote them." He narrowed his eyes. "Have you got something to admit, Mrs Churchill?"

"Well that depends. They do say that there's no smoke without fire."

"Does that mean to say the rumours about you at the garden party are true?"

"I will only say there's no smoke without fire. And no rain without clouds."

"No sunlight without sun," added Pemberley, warming to the theme.

"That's a good one," said Churchill. "You could say no moonlight without moon, too. No rain without... oh I just did that one. No clouds without rain."

"You can have clouds without rain," said Pemberley.

"Really?"

"Yes. It's often cloudy but not rainy. Cumulus clouds rarely produce rain, for example. Cumulonimbus, on the other hand, do. So you could say no rain without cumulonimbus clouds."

"Which wouldn't trip off the tongue particularly well." Churchill noticed the baffled expression on Smithy Miggins' face. "I suspect we're straying from the topic a little."

"So did you write the letter or did you not write the letter, Mrs Churchill?" asked the news reporter.

"Do I get it back if I say I did?"

"Let's say that you did write the letter, Mrs Churchill. I'd be willing to give it back to you if you allowed the *Compton Poppleford Gazette* the exclusive right to name you as the lady whose skirt fell down at the garden party."

"Why?"

"It would sell us some extra copies, that's for sure. It will all be tastefully done of course."

Churchill gave this some thought. Could she really cope with the embarrassment just to get her hands on the letter?

"Would it be a particularly prominent article?" she asked.

"Prominent enough for us to sell some extra copies."

"So on the front page then?"

"Probably. But there are no photographs of the incident so you're safe there. In fact, if you ask me, Mrs Churchill, I'd say there wasn't much more shame than being rescued from the tree in the cattle sling incident. And there was a picture with that one."

"Please don't remind me," she replied with an uncomfortable twinge in her stomach.

"So what do you say?"

"If I must."

"Must what?"

"I'd like my letter back please."

A grin spread across the reporter's face. "So it was you at the garden party, Mrs Churchill! I knew it."

"How did you know it?"

"That bit about the extra sandwiches."

Churchill clenched her jaw. "Can you fetch it for us please, Mr Miggins?"

"Course!" He dropped his cigarette onto the ground and stamped it out with the toe of his scuffed shoe. "That's the spirit, Mrs Churchill." He rubbed his hands together in glee. "Our readers are in for a treat!"

"I don't understand," whispered Pemberley as he walked off into the office. "Was it actually you at the garden party, Mrs Churchill?"

"Of course not," she hissed in reply. "But don't you see, Pembers? By admitting it's me, we get one of the letters which means that we can analyse the handwriting."

"Ah I see! Very clever indeed, Mrs Churchill."

"I don't mind enduring a bit of embarrassment if I can get my hands on some evidence, Pembers."

"But can you really face having your name plastered all

over the local paper, Mrs Churchill? People will have a field day."

"And they'll forget about it the next, Pembers. It will be worth it so that we have a chance of identifying the person behind the letter."

"And what if we don't? It will all have been for nothing."

"That's a risk I'll just have to take. And besides, we know the incident is entirely fictional anyway."

"Can we be sure of it?"

"Of course. Have we met anyone else who was at that same garden party who can verify the incident?"

"Come to think of it, no."

Smithy Miggins stepped out of the office with a notebook in his hand. He took a pencil from behind his ear as he approached them.

"Now then, Mrs Churchill, your letter gives me the bare bones of it. But perhaps you can flesh out the story a little for our readers. What colour was the skirt?"

"Are you going to give me back my letter, Mr Miggins?"

"Of course." He tapped his jacket pocket. "All in good time."

Back at their office, the two ladies surveyed the letter.

"So the question is, Pembers, has this letter been written by Mrs Bouton?"

"We need to see an example of her handwriting."

"Yes we do. Unless she disguised her hand when she wrote this."

Pemberley peered closely at the sharply slanting script through a magnifying glass. "The strokes are fluid," she commented, "which suggests the hand was moving at a relaxed and easy pace. The letters are consistently formed too. I'd say that the person who wrote this letter is comfortable writing in this manner. When someone is trying to disguise their handwriting there can be a few false marks, inconsistencies and a general halting manner about the script. They write slower and the characters are flooded with more ink. This person, however, has written fairly briskly. Look at the way the letter 't' is written, it's almost identical each time and has a sharp distinctive shape to it. There's nothing laboured about it at all."

"Well I must say that you have quite the analytical mind when it comes to examining handwriting, Pembers."

"Thank you Mrs Churchill, it was a skill which Atkins and I regularly practised."

"With good results as I can see. Are you one of these types who can describe an individual's personality through the style of their writing?"

"No. But I can say with certainty that this was written by a right-handed person. The pen has been pulled across the paper rather than pushed."

"Very good."

"I'd say there's some anger in this writing."

"Anger? Golly."

"Well, we know that the author is angry about the poor quality elastic and she's embarrassed that the vicar saw her petticoat. So that makes sense."

"Except the event is fictional."

"In which case she has imagined herself in the situation very well and the anger is showing in the handwriting."

"How?"

"The pressure on the pen is quite strong and the

upstrokes have a sharp angle to them. It's been written at speed too."

"So the handwriting seems quite authentic, which is odd when you consider it's describing a fictional event."

"The author of this letter has only disguised their handwriting a little, perhaps not at all. I've seen plenty of letters written in a disguised hand and there's often a clumsiness about them, unless they've been written by a master forger."

"Which is unlikely."

"Perhaps Mrs Bouton is a master forger?"

"If she was, Pembers, she'd be in a big city somewhere plying her craft and earning lots of money."

"Maybe she's lying low in Compton Poppleford?"

"I can't deny people have lied low here before. But that said, I don't think Mrs Bouton is one of them. She's too good at being a haberdasher. That's what she spends her time on and that's why her shop is so successful."

"Well she could have just scribbled out this letter without caring that it was in her own handwriting. As a newcomer to the village, she would have perhaps assumed that no one knew what her handwriting was like. There are some spelling mistakes too."

"Are there?"

"Petticoat and embarrassment are spelt wrong."

"Interesting. It makes you wonder what the other letters are like, doesn't it Pembers? Are they all written in the same handwriting?"

"Smithy Miggins surely wouldn't fall for that."

"You'd hope not. I'd like to get my hands on them."

"I'm not pretending to be the woman whose drawers almost fell down if that's what you're suggesting, Mrs Churchill."

"I wouldn't dare. It would be good to have someone

claim it for us though, wouldn't it? I wonder if there's a man who'd pretend to admit he had crumpled socks at the golf club dinner."

"I think we have enough work trying to identify the writer of this letter, Mrs Churchill."

"Yes we do, you're right. And the next step is to find out what Mrs Bouton's handwriting is like. There's a possibility that she disguised it, but if she didn't then it would be wonderful to catch her out, wouldn't it?"

"How do we get an example of her handwriting?"

"Good question, Pembers. That's the tricky bit."

Chapter 25

"I'VE GOT a plan for getting an example of Mrs Bouton's handwriting," said Pemberley as Churchill arrived in the office the following morning.

"Marvellous Pembers! How do we do it?"

"We ask her to write something."

"Well I'd say that was rather obvious. Is there more to the plan?"

"Oh yes, we can't just ask her to write something down can we? It would make her suspicious. We need to get her to write down an order of some sort. We could request some obscure buttons or ribbon that she'll need to order for us and, in doing so, she'll have to write something down. She'll give us a bit of paper with the order written on it and then we can match it to the letter we've obtained."

"What an excellent idea, Pembers. The only drawback being the fact that we'll end up spending more money in that woman's shop. Mrs Thonnings won't be pleased."

"Well we can explain that it's a necessary evil so that we can conduct a thorough investigation."

"Very good, Pembers. I like that explanation. All we need to do then is come up with something obscure which she's unlikely to have in stock."

"Handmade shell buttons should do it I think."

"Handmade shell buttons would cost a pretty penny, Pembers! Can't we come up with something unusual yet affordable?"

"Well the two are often mutually exclusive."

"You're not wrong there. This could be a puzzle."

"Perhaps we could send her a letter and then she'll need to write us a reply?"

"And what would the letter be about?"

"We could make an enquiry about something, perhaps we could ask her if she has a certain type of ribbon in stock?"

"Won't she think it odd that we're writing to her instead of visiting her shop which is five minutes' walk from here?"

"Yes she probably will, but at least we'll have an example of her handwriting."

"Let's give it some more thought after we've had our elevenses, Pemberley. I find I'm much better at hatching plans once I've had my elevenses. Now, in the meantime, we need to update our incident board after yesterday's kerfuffle.

The two ladies spent a pleasant morning rearranging their incident board and enjoying tea and freshly baked currant buns. They were just about to pause for lunch when they heard a visitor on the stairs. Tryphena bustled into the room, one arm in a sling.

"My goodness, whatever happened Tryph?" asked Churchill, getting to her feet.

"Oh it's nothing to make a fuss about. Just a burnt hand."

"A burnt hand? How awful." Churchill made her way around to the other side of the desk and positioned a chair for her visitor. "You must sit down and have a rest."

"I'm not an invalid Annabel! My hand received a little toasting in the library fire, that's all. It will be as right as rain in a week. Now have a look in here." She plonked an old, battered handbag on Churchill's desk.

"What is it?"

"Open it up and find out."

Churchill did as she was told. Inside the handbag were a few tatty pieces of paper. As Churchill pulled them out, she saw that the edges were singed and blackened.

"Golly, does this have something to do with your burnt hand?"

"It certainly does. Now unfold the papers and you'll see that what you have there is the will we've all been looking for."

"The second will, Tryphena? How exciting!"

"Well part of it, anyway. The rest was burned to a crisp."

"Oh dear." Churchill lay out the singed pieces on her desk and spotted Gertie's signature alongside Mr Porge's. The date was the twenty-eighth of May which fitted with Mr Porge telling them the will had been signed at the end of May.

"So what does it say?" asked Churchill, her eyes skimming over the densely typed text. "Who did he leave his estate to?"

"Well I got his watch, shirt studs and shirt pins."

"And the estate?"

"Cairistiona got his library of books and prints."

"But what about the rest of it Tryph? Who is the main beneficiary?"

"Oh I don't know, that bit burned in the fire."

Churchill gave a sigh and sank down into her chair. "How did it even end up in the fire?" she asked.

"Well I was walking past the library shortly after breakfast this morning when I heard an unmistakeable crackle. Now the fire isn't lit in there until four o'clock in the afternoon."

"You instantly knew something was afoot!"

"I certainly did! I stepped into the room just in time to see Mrs Surpant hurling some papers into the fire. Well I knew there was something instantly suspicious about that, so I darted over to the fireplace and yanked them back out again."

"I can't imagine she was happy about that."

"Of course she wasn't. 'Give me those!' she cried out at me and I dashed from that room quicker than a foxhound after a fox."

"Poor fox," lamented Pemberley.

"There wasn't actually a fox, Miss Pemberley," said Churchill. "Did the housekeeper give chase, Tryphena?"

"She tried, but then she went skidding about on her well-polished floor."

"Well that is a shame indeed."

"I shall inform Inspector Mappin about what she's done of course, she was willingly attempting to destroy a will which was dated later than the one she had been named in."

"Is she named in this will at all?"

"Not that I can see."

"Interesting. So we can only assume that she wasn't named in this burnt will and that's the reason you found her trying to destroy it."

"Exactly. Furthermore, she will know who's been named in the will."

"Of course!"

"And I can't say that I fancy trying to extract the information from her. Would you mind trying, Mrs Churchill?"

The thought was as appealing to Churchill as consuming a bowl of cold porridge.

"How do we know she'll tell me the truth?" she replied.

"Well there's a thought…" Tryphena considered this. "She might tell you the truth or she might make it up, mightn't she? She could say whoever she liked! Oh darn it."

Churchill examined the scraps of the burnt will again. "Please could you bring your magnifying glass over here, Miss Pemberley?"

Her assistant did as she asked.

"I want to find a reference to the law firm which drafted this will," said Churchill. "If we can find out who it is then surely they'll have a copy, don't you think?"

"A great idea!" replied Tryphena.

"There's something at the top here," said Pemberley, peering closely through her magnifying glass. "Bin B."

"Binby? Where, Miss Pemberley?"

"It's 'bin' and then a comma then the capital letter B."

"Does binby make any sense to you, Tryphena?" asked Churchill.

"None at all."

"Let's make a list of the law firms in the village," said Churchill, picking up pencil and paper. "First of all there's Mr Verney's outfit and then, who else?" Pemberley and Tryphena stared at her blankly. "Don't either of you know any more law firms in the village?" she asked.

They both shook their heads. "Law firms are terribly dull places," said Pemberley. "I don't pay attention to them as a rule."

"Right." Churchill dropped her pencil onto her desk.

"You know what this means, don't you? We'll have to go down to the library and examine the telephone directory."

"Oh but I can't," said Pemberley.

"Why not?"

"I have to hide from Mrs Higginbath."

"Have you not returned that book about rocks yet?"

"No, I keep forgetting. The fine will already have reached a halfpenny."

"Oh dear. Well why don't you fetch the book now so that we can take it back, apologise, pay the fine and then have a look at the telephone directory?"

"No I can't, Mrs Higginbath will tell me off. That's another reason I haven't returned the book yet, I can't face the telling-off I'll get when I walk in there with it."

"Can't you put it through the letterbox of an evening with the fine and a note of apology in an attached envelope?" suggested Tryphena.

"I suppose I could. There's no stopping her hunting me down and giving me the telling-off even after I've returned the book."

"Well it seems that the longer you leave it, the crosser she's going to get, Miss Pemberley," said Churchill. "So you just need to be big and brave and march into that library with the book and your ha'penny. Now none of this is getting us any closer to discovering who this binby law firm is. Do you have a reading ticket for the library, Tryph?"

"Yes I do."

"Excellent, then let's pop down there now and look in the telephone directory."

"Do you not have a reading ticket, Annabel?"

"No I don't. It's a long story but, in summary, Mrs Higginbath doesn't like me very much."

"Oh dear, poor you. It's not nice to be on the wrong side of Mrs Higginbath."

"Exactly," said Pemberley. "That's why I'm too scared to return the library book."

Chapter 26

"Too terrified to show her face is she?" sneered Mrs Higginbath as Churchill stepped into the library with Tryphena. The square-faced librarian sat at her desk, her thick-fingered hands interlocked and resting next to a sign bearing her name.

"I'm sorry but I don't know what you're talking about, we're here to look up something in the telephone directory," replied Churchill.

"You know I'm talking about Miss Pemberley," replied the librarian. "*Notable Rock Formations in Shropshire* was due back four days ago."

"Can you recall the exact title of every overdue book, Mrs Higginbath?"

"I certainly can. And I know who's got it and how overdue it is."

"Well good for you. Right, we're just off to have a nose in the telephone directory."

"I don't believe you have a reading ticket, Mrs Churchill."

"No I haven't, but I'm accompanying my good friend

Tryphena here for it is she who wishes to look up something."

"As long as it's her looking something up and not you, Mrs Churchill."

"Of course, I'm merely her assistant. She requires my help because she has one arm in a sling."

"And tell Miss Pemberley that she's only making matters worse for herself."

"Must I be the bearer of such unfortunate news?"

"I'm afraid you'll have to be Mrs Churchill, seeing as she's giving me a wide berth at the moment."

"Rest assured, Mrs Higginbath, that I shall remind her that you'd like your important rock book back."

Churchill and Tryphena made their way to the back of the library.

"The irony, Tryph, is that once Miss Pemberley returns that book it will merely sit on a shelf in here gathering dust for the next year. I can't imagine anyone else being remotely interested in it at all. Rocks in Shropshire? The place must be at least two hundred miles from here."

"I can hear you!" called out Mrs Higginbath.

"Crikey," muttered Churchill. "The woman has super-natural powers."

"I can still hear you!"

Once the two ladies had found the telephone directory, they began looking up the law firms.

"Marjoribanks and Courtney," said Tryphena. "They sound rather grand don't they?"

"Doesn't fit with binby. We need bin, a comma and a capital B."

"A comma, eh? We've got Buxton, Buxton and Wilmot."

"Doesn't sound like the one we're after."

"Knobble and Bone. I don't think Daddy would have

plumped for them, they sound rather downmarket. Meldon Milbank, no comma there. Selwin, Postlethwaite, Duncan and Newtoes. Two commas! Any good?"

"No."

"Charters. Just the one name. Charters. I like that. Fletcher and Fitzmaurice. Now I have a distant cousin who's a Fitzmaurice, I wonder if there's any relation between them?"

Churchill felt a ball of impatience begin to grow in her chest. "May I have a look at the list myself, Tryphena?"

But her friend didn't appear to hear her. "Bailey and Foxfoot. Now that is unusual, do you think Foxfoot is an actual surname? Walpoles. I like that one. A nice traditional name, Walpoles. Delightful, don't you think?"

"Please can I look at the list, Tryphena? The quicker we find this company, the quicker we can speak to them and find out who's inherited your father's estate."

"Oh yes, of course. Erm…. Where did I get to? Foxfoot wasn't it? No, Walpoles. Are you trying to snatch the directory from me, Mrs Churchill?"

"Yes," she replied through gritted teeth. She gave the list a glance and willed her trained detective eye to spot the correct law firm. "Dobbin, Bapp and Pringle," she announced. "That'll do."

"Where are they?"

"Dorchester by the looks of things, let's make a note of their telephone number." Churchill scribbled it down into her notebook.

"Dobbin, Bapp and Pringle? I've never heard of them."

"There's a 'bin', a comma and a capital B."

"I'm sure Daddy would have mentioned them."

"I think there were quite a few things Daddy didn't mention."

"Such as what?"

"Such as how many wills he made, for one. Now come along, Tryphena, we've got work to do."

⟋

"Off anywhere exciting?" asked Mrs Thonnings as Churchill, Pemberley, Oswald and Tryphena walked to the railway station.

"I don't know about exciting," replied Churchill. "We're off to a law firm in Dorchester."

"That sounds terribly important."

"It could be, we shall wait and see. That's only after we've endured the interminable journey on the branch line. But I have exciting news to impart to you about the elastic investigation when we return, Mrs Thonnings."

"Oh really!" The haberdasher's face lit up. "I didn't think you'd find the time to do any work on it."

"Oh we've found time all right. And yours truly has also made a bit of a personal sacrifice too."

"Really? You've sacrificed yourself, Mrs Churchill? I'm sure there was no need to go to such extremes."

"All will become apparent in a day or two, Mrs Thonnings." Churchill felt an uncomfortable twinge as she considered the imminent publication of the fictional newspaper report about her skirt embarrassment. "But rest assured, we have a plan in place!"

"Well that's wonderful to hear." Mrs Thonnings beamed.

"Now haven't you got a shop to be tending to?"

"Well yes, I suppose I have."

"There could be customers waiting."

"I doubt it. Have fun at the law firm!"

"I wonder if anyone has ever had any fun in a law firm?" pondered Churchill as they continued on their way.

"Oh they must have!" replied Tryphena. "You appear to have quite a low opinion of lawyers, Annabel, but some of them can be wonderful fun indeed!"

Chapter 27

"OH DEAR, oh dear. The probate registry will take a dim view of this." The grey-haired, grey-suited Mr Dobbin, of Dobbin, Bapp and Pringle, gave a slow shake of his head as he surveyed the burnt scraps of paper arranged neatly on his desk.

"Is the will still valid?" asked Tryphena hopefully.

A dry, mocking sound came from the back of the solicitor's throat. Churchill surmised it was supposed to be a laugh.

"No. Not valid in this state I'm afraid."

"Do you have a copy?" asked Churchill.

"Do we have a copy?"

"That's what I just asked you."

"I would have to look in the files."

"So can you look in the files for us?"

"In due course I probably can, yes."

"Would it trouble you to look in the files sooner than due course? For instance, now?"

"Are you in a great hurry?"

"The matter of the Earl of Middlemop's will has

caused some consternation in the Ridley-Balls family. It's something which needs to be resolved as quickly as possible."

The dry, mocking sound came again. "Well that's often the way in these cases. Especially when there's a lot of money and a large estate involved."

"You are aware that the Earl was murdered?" asked Churchill.

"Yes I heard that."

"And we believe the motive had something to do with his will. We've already had one will read out and the beneficiary of that will was found trying to destroy this will which would have superseded it. There's an awful lot of skulduggery going on and we need to get to the bottom of it."

"It's a criminal offence to intentionally destroy a will," announced the solicitor.

"We're aware of that and we'll get our local constabulary onto the case, for what it's worth. It's also a criminal offence to murder someone and that is why Miss Ridley-Balls, here, has employed me, here, and Miss Pemberley, there, to investigate. Now your urgent cooperation with this matter is appreciated, Mr Dobbin. Especially as there's only one train an hour on the branch line after six o'clock this evening. We'd like to get home in good time."

"Well I can ask Bapp Junior to look in the files."

"Good, thank you." A long silence followed as everyone waited for someone else to speak. "Are you going to ask Bapp Junior now?" ventured Churchill.

"I can do, if he's not busy doing something else."

"Wonderful, well let's hope he's not busy doing something else because that really would put a spanner in the works, wouldn't it?"

"I shall ask him now." The solicitor rose from his desk and left the office.

"Am I the only person who's resisting the urge to pull every hair out of their head in sheer frustration?" fumed Churchill while Mr Dobbin was gone. "The man is intolerable! Why on earth did your father use this firm, Tryph?"

"I have no idea. And curses on that Mrs Surpant woman for destroying Daddy's will! She should be locked up and left to rot!"

"Not a pleasant fate."

"She deserves it!"

"I say yes to locking up, but the rotting part is maybe a step too far."

The solicitor returned. "Bapp Junior is looking in the files."

"Excellent. Thank you."

"So if you will excuse me, I have some conveyancing to be getting on with."

"Is there somewhere we can wait while Bapp Junior is looking in the files?"

"Wait?"

"Yes, we would like to wait. Is there a room we can convey ourselves to while you're conveyancing?"

"Well you can sit in with Miss Brown."

The three ladies spent the next hour squashed together on three chairs in the secretary's tiny office. The ceaseless rat-tat-tat of the typewriter drummed into their heads yet Oswald dozed peacefully on Pemberley's lap.

"How long can it possibly take Bapp Junior to find a file?" grumbled Tryphena for the seventh time.

"And still no one has offered us any tea," added

Churchill, staring pointedly at Miss Brown behind her typewriter.

Eventually a young man with pimpled skin appeared.

"Found it!" he announced, cheerfully waving a large envelope in his hand.

"Thank goodness," said Churchill. The three ladies scrambled to get out of their seats.

"Bapp Senior will only speak to Miss Ridley-Balls," said the youth.

"Oh will he?" replied Churchill. Her chair gave an alarming creak as she fell back onto it with resignation. Miss Brown startled.

"Is it all right?" she asked.

"Is what all right?"

"The chair."

"Yes, the chair's fine. I'm sure it will appreciate you asking after it. So refreshing to meet someone concerned about the welfare of chairs, wouldn't you say, Miss Pemberley? Never mind the poor old ladies who've been condemned to sit on them for hour after hour, a creeping numbness slowly enveloping their sit-upons. And without so much as an offer of a cup of tea or slice of cake. It's quite a scandal, wouldn't you say, Miss Pemberley?"

"What are you doing out here?" asked Tryphena, as she stepped out of the offices of Dobbin, Bapp and Pringle fifteen minutes later.

"Mrs Churchill was asked to leave," said Pemberley.

"Why?"

"It seems that Miss Brown is of a sensitive disposition," replied Churchill. "Easily offended, by all accounts. I prefer it out here actually, the air is fresher and there's no typewriter. Now what did Bapp Senior have to say?"

"Well he recalled drawing up the will with Daddy and we looked through the copy which Bapp Junior found."

"And?"

"Humphrey's got it all."

"Golly, really?"

"Yes, really."

"He was the expected heir though, wasn't he?"

"Yes, I suppose he was."

"So for some reason your father changed his mind about Mrs Surpant being the beneficiary. She's not going to be happy is she? She's going to be in trouble for attempting to destroy the will too."

"And left to rot," added Pemberley.

"Well not necessarily that bit. But, overall, it's good news, wouldn't you say, Tryph? Surely Humphrey is better than Mrs Surpant? It means that things stay in the family."

"Well I don't know about that. Humphrey's not really family you see."

"But that's all just rumour, isn't it? Your Aunt Nora told us all about the basket weavers, I can't say that I believe the tale."

"Well I do! Humphrey is a changeling and that's that. It's not right that he should inherit Daddy's estate. Not right at all!"

Chapter 28

"WE SPENT the whole afternoon with Tryphena Ridley-Balls yesterday," said Pemberley as she and Churchill drank tea in their office the following day. "And you didn't once ask her about the inconsistencies in her statement."

"What inconsistencies?"

"Don't tell me you've forgotten, Mrs Churchill? Both Mrs Surpant and Cairistiona say she was arguing with the Earl by the fountain that afternoon and yet Tryphena has made no mention of it."

"That's not an inconsistency as such, Pembers, I expect she just forgot about it."

"Well I think that if I'd had a heated argument with my father on the day he was murdered then I would remember it. I would feel immensely guilty that I'd had a terrible row with him on the day he'd died."

"Well that's just you, Pembers."

"And most other people! Whether she's purposefully declined to mention it or not, don't you think you should ask her about it? There's also the possibility that Mrs Surpant and Cairistiona aren't being truthful. Perhaps there was no argument at all and that's why Tryphena hasn't mentioned it. It needs to be ironed out, Mrs Churchill."

"Very well. I shall iron it out."

"Are you sure you will? I know it can't be easy when Tryphena's your friend."

"The fact she's my friend, Pembers, is neither here nor there. When I have my detective hat on then all alliances are pushed to one side."

"You have a detective hat? I don't think I've seen that before."

"I was speaking metaphorically, Pembers. Although I must say that I do like the idea of us getting detective hats. They would make us look more official wouldn't they? I wonder if the local milliner would make some for us?"

"Perhaps she would make one for Oswald too?"

"Well that would be simply delightful! He would be thoroughly adorable wouldn't he? Oh hello, Mrs Thonnings! I didn't even hear you coming up the stairs."

"I tiptoed," replied the red-haired lady. Churchill glanced uneasily at the newspaper in her hand.

"Why on earth did you tiptoe?"

"Just to see if I could catch you out."

"Do we need catching out?"

"I don't know. I suppose it was a little game I came up with on a whim. Anyway, I've just read your exclusive story in the newspaper, Mrs Churchill, and I must say I'm rather confused."

"So it's in there then."

"Yes. Page one, page two, and pages four to seven."

"It's unfortunate that nothing else of major importance has happened in the village in the past day or so, I had hoped it would be pushed to the back of the paper."

"You give a detailed account of your skirt slipping

down at the garden party, Mrs Churchill, but didn't we decide that the entire account had been made up by Mrs Bouton?"

"Yes we did and that is still the case. I had to pretend to Smithy Miggins at the *Compton Poppleford Gazette* that I had written the poison elastic letter so that he would give it to me. He drove a hard bargain, I'm afraid, and I was forced to give him a false account of the fictional incident in return for the letter."

"Can a fictional account be false?" asked Pemberley.

"Probably. Yes, no. I don't know, Pembers. You're confusing matters."

"So this is the sacrifice you mentioned yesterday?" asked Mrs Thonnings.

"Absolutely."

"You sacrificed your reputation?"

"Well I hope my reputation hasn't received that much damage. We were reaching the point where everyone, for some reason, thought the unfortunate lady at the garden party was me anyway. Better just to pretend that it was and get my mitts on the letter."

"But it's quite embarrassing."

"What's a little embarrassment? I'm not ashamed of it."

Mrs Thonnings peered at the newspaper and read out, "'The vicar, and his assembled guests, got more than they bargained for when buxom Mrs Churchill decided that one serving of ham and tongue sandwiches was not enough.'"

"There's no need for the word buxom."

"'No sooner had she reached for her second plateful when the twang of pinging elastic echoed around the neatly manicured gardens,'" continued Mrs Thonnings. "'All heads turned to witness Mrs Churchill's skirt slithering to the ground revealing her silken petticoats.' Oh goodness, Mrs Churchill, don't you feel discomfort hearing this?"

"Yes, there is some marginal discomfort." Churchill shifted in her seat. "Is that all?"

"Oh no, there are columns of it! There are descriptions of your red face and fumbling fingers as you haul your skirt back up again, it goes on and on."

"Right, well I think we've all heard enough for now. The important thing is that we have the letter."

"May I see it?"

"Of course."

Churchill found the letter in her drawer and passed it to Mrs Thonnings, wondering whether it had been worth the embarrassment after all.

"Well I suppose this letter doesn't provide anything more than what's already been reported," said the haberdasher once she had finished reading it.

"But do you recognise the handwriting?"

"Now you come to mention it, I think it does look vaguely familiar yes."

"You've seen it before?"

"I think so."

"So you've seen something which Mrs Bouton has written?"

"No I haven't."

"But we think this has been written by Mrs Bouton, don't we?"

"Yes, it must be!"

"So for this handwriting to look familiar, then you must have seen something Mrs Bouton has written."

"I see. Well maybe it just looks similar to some handwriting I saw once. I can't place it to be honest with you."

"And the handwriting could be forged," added Pemberley.

"Yes, there is that possibility," acknowledged Churchill. "However, Pemberley and I shall obtain a sample of Mrs Bouton's handwriting to compare it with. She may have written it in her own hand after all."

"Well I think it's an excellent plan and I think you're a very brave lady indeed, Mrs Churchill. Allowing the local newspaper to ridicule you just so that you could get hold of this letter. I really am truly grateful for everything you've done so far."

"Ridicule me?"

"Yes, you're a saint, you really are."

"Well that's very nice of you to say so, Mrs Thonnings. I shall ensure that I never read what's been written about me in today's *Compton Poppleford Gazette*."

"No, I wouldn't if I were you. How's the investigation into the Earl's murder going?"

"It's twisting and turning. There turned out to be a second will in which Humphrey Ridley-Balls is named as the inheritor of the estate. Better than the housekeeper I suppose."

"Oh I don't know about that. He's the son of the basket weavers."

"So the story goes, do you really believe that Mrs Thonnings?"

"Well we all believed it at the time. I'm not sure what the general thinking is now but he was never popular."

"Because of the basket weavers?"

"Yes."

"Did you ever hear where they disappeared to?"

"No. They simply disappeared."

"No one can really disappear to anywhere," added Pemberley. "If you can name a place they disappeared to then they haven't completely disappeared have they?"

"I don't think there's a need to examine my words

quite as closely as that, Pembers. Remember I am in discomfort from the news article, it won't take a lot to injure my feelings today. All I wished to do was establish whether or not anyone actually saw the basket weavers ever again."

"Not to my knowledge," replied Mrs Thonnings. "However I did hear word that they had something to do with the butler up at Gripedown Hall."

"Mr Porge?"

"I think that's the one."

"What did they have to do with him?"

"I think the basket weaver's wife was his sister or cousin. Something along those lines, but I could be wrong."

"Really? Mr Porge is related to the basket weavers?"

"Well you don't really know with these things, do you? Probably all just gossip and hearsay."

"The most reliable sources as far as I'm concerned, Mrs Thonnings."

Chapter 29

CHURCHILL GAVE Aunt Nora a wave from the driveway as they arrived at Gripedown Hall that afternoon. The old lady's face was visible at an upper window and Churchill could just about see her hand slowly raise in acknowledgement.

"Good afternoon, Inspector Mappin!" said Churchill cheerily, as they stepped into the entrance hall. He stood, notebook in hand, with Cairistiona. "And Mrs Vigors-Slipcote!" added Churchill. The inspector looked up from his notebook with a scowl.

"You're still investigating are you, Mrs Churchill?"

"We certainly are. Are you?"

"Of course I am, what a foolish question."

"Have you arrested Mrs Surpant yet for attempting to destroy the second will?"

"I've been informed about it."

"But not actually done anything about it?"

"This is a complicated investigation with many threads. I have every confidence that the necessary people will be apprehended in due course."

"Any suspects, Inspector?"

"That would be telling."

"Of course it would. Are you interested to know if we have any suspects, Inspector?"

"Do you?"

"That would be telling."

Inspector Mappin folded his notebook closed. "Well thank you for your time today, Mrs Vigors-Slipcote, I shall be in touch again shortly."

"Thank you, Inspector." She turned to Churchill and Pemberley. "What can I help you with ladies?"

"We're here to see Mr Porge."

"I believe it's his afternoon off," said Cairistiona.

"That's a shame."

"But if you need to see him urgently, Mrs Churchill, then his cottage is down at Sparrow's Bottom.

"Well thank you Mrs Vigors-Slipcote, we shall pay him a visit."

"I'm sure he'll appreciate that," said the inspector. "And it was very brave of you to allow the *Compton Popple-ford Gazette* to so publicly discuss your skirt mishap at the garden party, Mrs Churchill. I read it with great interest this morning."

Churchill tried to ignore the heat which was rushing to her face. "I'm pleased it provided you with a little enter-tainment, Inspector. Come along, Miss Pemberley, let's leave."

Mr Goldbeam was still tinkering with his motorcycle as the two ladies and their dog reached the row of little cottages huddled at Sparrow's Bottom. He gave them a nod of acknowledgement before hitting something on the machine with a small hammer.

"I say!" Churchill called out to him. "Which one is Mr Porge's?"

The handyman pointed at the cottage with the shiniest door and neatest window boxes.

"Thank you!"

Churchill lowered her voice as she and Pemberley approached the butler's home. "I suppose we needn't have asked, it's quite obvious that the tidiest cottage would be his. What on earth do you think Mrs Thonnings saw in Mr Goldbeam? That slack jaw of his is quite off-putting, wouldn't you say?"

"Perhaps he makes charming and intelligent conversation."

"I do admire your attempts to see the best in people, Pembers. Now let's find out what the butler has to say for himself. Perhaps we may see a different side to him now he's off-duty?"

Mr Porge had an apron tied around his waist when he answered the door. He also wore a brown sleeveless knitted pullover over brown slacks.

"Oh good afternoon, how different you look in civvies, Mr Porge!"

"What can I help you with?"

"We have a couple of questions to put to you if we may."

"I see."

As no invitation into his home was forthcoming, Churchill decided to press on while standing on the doorstep.

"We had a little chat with Mrs Vigors-Slipcote," she began. "And she told us that she witnessed an argument between your deceased employer and Miss Ridley-Balls by the statue on the day of his death. Was that something you witnessed?"

"It wasn't, no."

"Mrs Vigors-Slipcote informed us that she was in the drawing room when she witnessed this incident and when we asked her why she didn't intervene or speak to her father after the incident, she told us that she was waylaid by your good self, Mr Porge."

He gave a swallow. "I see."

"Do you recall the episode?"

"I recall speaking to Mrs Vigors-Slipcote in the drawing room that afternoon, yes."

"Jolly good, she told us that you'd back her up."

"I'm not backing anyone up, Mrs Churchill, merely confirming that I spoke to her in the drawing room that afternoon. I didn't realise at the time I was waylaying her, it's most unfortunate that I did so."

"She didn't seem particularly put out that you waylaid her so I wouldn't concern yourself about that. May I ask what the conversation was concerning?"

"It's rather difficult to remember now, it would have been some minor household matter of course."

"Of course. There's another little matter we'd like to discuss with you as well. I hear that the basket weavers who lived by the River Turnfork may have been some relations of yours. Well one of them, a sister or a cousin perhaps?"

His face stiffened. "I have no idea what you're talking about."

"The basket weavers? The supposed parents of Humphrey Ridley-Balls as some say?"

His hand moved to the door as if he wished to close it. "I pay no attention to such idle gossip."

"I'm not here to gossip, Mr Porge. I'm merely trying to establish if there is any truth in the rumour and, if you were related to the basket weavers, you perhaps could help shed some light on it?"

"I have no light to shed, Mrs Churchill. Now I must be getting on."

"Of course." Churchill felt another urge to chip away at his facade. "What will you be watching at the pictures this week, do you think?"

"I don't see why it's any concern of yours."

"Oh come now, Mr Porge, must you be so frosty? I'm only making friendly conversation. I realise that you don't like being asked questions but it's only little old me asking them. Surely we can find some familiar ground between us?" She said this with a wink which caused him to grip the door.

"If I can think of anything else I shall let you know, Mrs Churchill." He began to push the door closed.

"Oh please do," she replied through the decreasing gap. "I look forward to it!"

"What an odd man," she muttered to Pemberley as they walked away from the cottage. "It's useful that he verified Cairistiona's account in the drawing room but there was a flat refusal to discuss the basket weavers, wasn't there? I wonder why."

"He could be embarrassed to be related to people of a lower class."

"That's a very good explanation. But he could potentially be related to Humphrey Ridley-Balls, couldn't he? He could even be the man's uncle! I think it's time we visited the new ninth Earl of Middlemop at Loxley Grange. Where is Loxley Grange, Pembers?"

"I have no idea."

Chapter 30

"I'D BEEN WONDERING when you two ladies would pay me a visit and now here you are," said Humphrey Ridley-Balls with a beam.

"Here we are indeed!" chimed Churchill. "Were you really wondering when we'd pay you a visit?"

"Oh yes. As soon as Auntie Tryph said she'd engaged you to solve Grandpapa's murder, I began wondering when I'd have the opportunity to help. And now the moment's arrived!"

"It certainly has." Churchill sipped from a delicate bone china cup as she surveyed the opulent parlour and decided that, at this very moment, all was right with the world. Humphrey Ridley-Balls was proving himself to be a charming, entertaining host and Loxley Grange was exactly the sort of place she would like to live in.

The ninth earl had a raffish manner about him as he reclined on a chaise lounge. He wore a smart three piece suit but his tie was loosened a little. His dark, handsome looks tempted Churchill to think that she would have been quite attracted to him had she been born a few decades later.

"Well we must congratulate you on being the main beneficiary in your grandfather's will," she said.

"Oh, there's no need for that."

"But surely you must be pleased about it?"

"No it's all changed. A codicil has reared its ugly head."

"Ugh, that doesn't sound nice. I suppose these old houses can be prone to vermin infestations."

Humphrey broke out into a laugh. "Oh Mrs Churchill! What do you think I said?"

"I don't know. A cod thing or something with an ugly head."

He slapped his thigh and laughed some more.

"A codicil is an addition to a will, Mrs Churchill," said Pemberley.

"Oh, a codicil! Oh of course, silly me."

"You're a funny lady, Mrs Churchill," said Humphrey, wiping a tear of mirth from his eye.

"Do you think so?"

"Oh yes. Great value as they say."

"Well thank you, I aim to please. Now this codicil. Where was it and what did it say?"

"Well Auntie Carrie found it in some of Grandpapa's papers and the long and the short of it is that everything now goes to Auntie Tryph."

"Golly, really?"

"Yes."

"Poor you, my lord."

"Oh call me Humphrey."

"But you're an earl."

"Which is all a lot of fuss and nonsense if you ask me."

"So now Tryphena gets everything," pondered

Churchill. "What a turn out for the books. Mr Porge didn't tell us that earlier, did he Miss Pemberley?"

"Mr Porge probably didn't know," said Humphrey. "The situation seems to be changing every day. It will probably be someone else tomorrow!"

"It probably will. Your grandfather appears to have changed his will as often as he changed his undergarments."

"Oh how funny, Mrs Churchill. More often, I'd say!"

"Goodness, really?" Churchill wrinkled her nose and Humphrey slapped his thigh with laughter again.

"Shall we get on with the questions we were going to ask?" ventured Pemberley.

"Ah yes, I suppose we should. When did you last see your grandfather, Humphrey?"

"About a fortnight before he died. I visited Gripedown for dinner. Although he didn't dine with us as such. He sat with us during the soup course and then took himself off to have supper in his room."

"I see. And did you visit Gripedown Hall again before his death?"

"No, that was the last time until I attended the reading of the will earlier this week. Rather a farce that turned out to be!"

"Well wasn't it? And now we have a coddy whatsit that really does make a mockery of it all. I wonder, Humphrey, if we may address a rather sensitive matter."

"Of course."

"The matter of your parentage. There's a rather silly story, which has done the rounds for many years it seems, which claims that your parents are actually basket weavers."

"That's right."

Churchill felt reassured by his calm and measured response to the topic.

"What are your views on the story, if you don't mind me asking, that is?"

"Well I prefer to believe that it's a silly story with no truth in it whatsoever. My father was Horace Ridley-Balls and my mother was his dear wife, Delilah. It is odd, however, that they decided to go walking in the woods when my birth was imminent. However, that's what they decided to do and the decision has led to me being treated as an outcast by the rest of my family ever since."

"Oh poor you, Humphrey!"

"Oh don't worry about me, Mrs Churchill, I'm a big strong lad and I've grown quite used to it. I live a happy life here with my beautiful wife and our delightful children and I couldn't wish for anything more."

"Well that's lovely to hear." Churchill couldn't help feeling a little envious of the beautiful wife. "And what did your grandfather make of the rumours?"

"He thought they were complete nonsense. He considered me his true heir."

"Well that is nice. We also heard a little rumour that the basket weavers were some relation of Mr Porge."

"I believe that to be true, I met them once."

Churchill felt her jaw drop.

"You *met* them? Really? When?"

"Oh I was just a little lad, ma and pa were still alive. We were at Gripedown and I was running about the place, as little lads do. I happened to see old Porgy with a couple, they were on the track near Sparrow's Bottom. They smiled at me and said 'hello' and what have you. I didn't think a great deal of it but I happened to mention it to Nanny and she told me they were Porge's sister and her husband and that they were the basket weavers."

"The basket weavers who everyone claimed had completely vanished?"

"They vanished after that, I never saw them again."

"And how long ago was that?"

"It would have been about thirty years ago. More than that probably."

"Golly. Did you ever learn their names?"

"Roger and Dora Pipwaite."

"How nice to finally learn their names. And it's possible that Mr Porge kept up a correspondence with his sister, Dora."

"Perhaps he did. I couldn't tell you, Mrs Churchill. Had I ever considered them to be my parents then I would have thought about it some more but I haven't."

"Golly, well Mr Porge flatly denied he was any relation to them, didn't he, Miss Pemberley? What a shame he couldn't bring himself to tell us the truth."

"That's Porge for you, he's rather stiff."

"But why would he deny it?"

"I really couldn't tell you. Embarrassment, perhaps? Or maybe he's protecting his sister. If people knew where she was now then all the old rumours would resurface again, not that they ever went too far below the surface in the first place. I suspect she'd be hounded."

"Well Mr Porge's secret would be safe with us, wouldn't it, Miss Pemberley?"

"Absolutely."

"If you ask me, Mrs Churchill, the man's a fool for refusing to confide in two ladies as delightful as yourselves."

"Oh thank you for saying so my lord, I mean, Humphrey. How very kind of you." Churchill took another sip of tea. "May I ask, Humphrey, who you think could have poisoned your grandfather?"

"I really couldn't say, Mrs Churchill. For one thing, I struggle to believe that anyone could bring themselves to do something so awful. I prefer to think that it was a terrible accident. Perhaps Grandpapa happened across some cyanide and put it in his medicine as some sort of experiment?"

"That would be a very strange thing to do."

"Well it would, wouldn't it? But perhaps he didn't realise it was cyanide?"

"Even so, it would be odd to put an unknown substance into one's remedy syrup."

"Ah, but perhaps it was labelled as something else? Perhaps the poison had been stored in another bottle or packet of some sort? Maybe it was labelled as aspirin?"

"That's a very interesting thought indeed, Humphrey. We haven't considered this, have we Miss Pemberley? Although, if the cyanide had been labelled as something else, surely the packet would have been found by now?"

"If the police have done their job properly, yes."

"Oh well, that's a good point too Humphrey. Between you and ourselves, we don't have much faith in the capabilities of Inspector Mappin. The police are usually quite capable of doing their job of course, I don't like to tar them all with the same brush. I was married to the wonderful Detective Chief Inspector Churchill of the Metropolitan Police for forty years."

"Were you really, Mrs Churchill?"

"I was." She gave a proud smile.

"Well he must have been a worthy man indeed."

"Oh he was. He would have had this case solved in no time whatsoever. And he would have adored you too, Humphrey."

"Would he really?" He gave a flattered smile.

"Oh yes, he would."

"Have we got any more questions for the Earl, Mrs Churchill?" interrupted Pemberley.

Churchill pulled her gaze away from him for a moment to consider.

"No... that's all I can think of for the time being."

"So who's on your list?" asked Humphrey.

"My list?"

"The suspects." He gave a wink. "Who needs to be looking over their shoulder as far as Mrs Churchill's concerned?"

"Oh, that list."

"Have you got another list?"

"I've got many lists, Humphrey."

"Have you indeed? Now I am intrigued." He gave a charming grin.

"The Earl asked you about the suspects, Mrs Churchill," said Pemberley impatiently. "After you've told him, perhaps we can leave?"

"Must we be in such a hurry, Miss Pemberley? I must say that I'm quite enjoying drinking tea in the Earl's parlour."

"We have a murder case to be getting on with."

"Yes we do. Please excuse my assistant, Humphrey, she doesn't like to be kept sitting about."

"I completely understand, I'm not the sort of chap who sits about either. Every morning I get up with the lark and take a swim in my lake."

"Do you indeed? Well that is interesting." Churchill was just considering this sight when Pemberley interrupted her thoughts with a cough.

"The suspects?" she said. "Well anyone who was able to access your grandpapa's room that day. So we have Mrs Surpant, Mr Porge, Gertie and Mr Goldbeam the handyman who visited to unblock the chimney."

"Not Gertie," said Humphrey. "I don't think for one minute she would do such a thing."

"Well me neither," replied Churchill. "But we will have to consider the possibility until we have enough evidence to rule her out. An unsavoury thought, I know. But it's the detective's way."

"Of course."

"And then, equally unsavoury, is the possibility of my dear friend, Tryph. Your aunt of course. I really don't like to consider her but... evidence and all that. And there's your other aunt too, Cairistiona."

Humphrey pursed his lips as he considered this. "My money's on Surpant," he said. "Although Porge is a good possibility too if you consider the possibility of revenge."

"Revenge?"

"Yes, for his sister being sent away. There's a story that Grandpapa had them banished. He was tired of the silly rumours and hoped their disappearance would be the end of it."

"Golly," said Churchill. "Banished? Well I could imagine Mr Porge being rather annoyed about that."

Chapter 31

"So here we are, Pembers, the River Turnfork. Quite a pretty little spot isn't it?" A weeping willow dipped its branches into the slow moving water and the warm air was filled with birdsong. Sheep grazed in emerald green fields beyond the river and Oswald snuffled among the reeds at the side of the path. "Now where's the basket weavers' cottage?"

"About half a mile up this way," said Pemberley. "If my memory serves me."

"You've been here before?"

"Not to purposefully visit the cottage, but Mrs Higgin-bath and I passed it when we were walking the length of the River Turnfork many years ago."

"Gosh, what on earth possessed you to do that?"

"It was something we used to do when we were young."

"It must have taken you weeks!"

"No, not that long at all. The River Turnfork is quite short."

"I see. Well we have an hour before Mr Speakman

returns to collect us, so let's make the most of it. Murder investigations can sometimes be fun, can't they Pembers? There aren't many jobs where you can enjoy a nice stroll by the river as part of your work."

The two ladies began walking. "How lovely it was to sit and chat with the ninth Earl of Middlemop, Pembers. Can you believe he's an earl? A fine young man in possession of a great deal of intelligence. He doesn't seem like the rest of the family."

"He doesn't, you can see where the rumours started," replied Pemberley. "And it's interesting that he doesn't believe that the basket weavers were his parents, don't you think?"

"I suppose he would like to think that he's a Ridley-Ball."

"Ridley-Balls."

"But it doesn't seem right to say he's a Ridley-Balls, a Ridley-Ball sounds better don't you think?"

"It does, but it's not correct."

"Oh Pembers, we don't have to be correct all the time do we? It can be terribly dull."

The two ladies paused to watch a family of swans gliding past.

"I thought it was rather interesting that Humphrey actually met the basket weavers," continued Churchill. "I wonder if the meeting was engineered by them? Perhaps they knew he was their son and they wanted to see him before the Earl made them disappear. And another thought occurs to me, can we really be sure that the Earl banished them?"

"I'm not sure the Earl even had the right to banish them."

"No, it sounds like the sort of thing they did in medieval times."

"But it could explain why they suddenly disappeared," replied Pemberley. "And I could understand Mr Porge being annoyed about it."

"Yes, if the Earl forced the basket weavers to move away then Mr Porge would have been rather resentful of that wouldn't he? Given that the basket weaver's wife was his sister. It seems now that Mr Porge had both the opportunity and the motive to poison the Earl."

"But if he did decide to have his revenge on the Earl," said Pemberley, "then why wait over thirty years?"

"An interesting point, maybe it took him that long to pluck up the courage?"

"And what about Humphrey Ridley-Balls himself? Perhaps he murdered his grandfather?"

"Quite impossible, Pembers! I can't imagine him having done such a thing. What would he have to gain by it?"

"Well he was named as the beneficiary in the Earl's second will, maybe he decided to murder the Earl while he knew he was the beneficiary. Or perhaps he decided to murder the Earl because the basket weavers were his parents after all, and he was upset that the Earl banished them."

"So, you're suggesting, Pembers, that both Humphrey and Mr Porge had a motive for murdering the Earl, that motive being the fact the Earl banished the basket weavers?"

"Yes. And perhaps the two of them colluded?" suggested Pemberley. "It's unlikely that Humphrey Ridley-Balls put the poison into his grandfather's medicine himself because he wasn't seen at Gripedown Hall that day. However, he could have asked Mr Porge to do the deed for him."

"Yes, that's a good point Pembers, and let's not forget

that Gertie had access to the Earl's rooms and was regularly in and out during the day. We haven't yet found a possible motive for Gertie; however, she could have been asked to put the poison in the remedy syrup for someone else."

"It's difficult to imagine Gertie doing such a thing."

"I agree with you Pembers, but Humphrey could be quite persuasive don't you think? And maybe she didn't realise it was cyanide and he told her that it was something else instead. Or what if she had been threatened with losing her job or some other possible scandal could be unearthed? Someone could have bribed or blackmailed her into doing such a thing."

"What an awful thing to do to Gertie!"

"Dreadful."

"And notice how Humphrey was adamant that Gertie couldn't have put the poison in his grandfather's remedy syrup. Perhaps he knows it was her and was trying to steer us away from suspecting her?"

"Well he's underestimated us in that case, Pembers. Oh, I can't believe we're thinking such ill things of Gertie and Humphrey! It couldn't be true, could it?"

A hedge rose along one side of the path and Churchill could make out a crumbling stone wall alongside it. Looking ahead, she saw a brown mound with weeds growing on it. Then she realised she was looking at the collapsed roof of a thatched cottage. There were two little windows and a small red door and the cottage's cracked, white walls were covered in green lichen.

"Could this be it Pembers?"

"Yes it is."

"How sad that the little cottage has fallen into such a state. It must have been very pretty here once. The basket weavers must have been extremely sad to leave it."

The two ladies sat themselves on a section of broken stone wall and contemplated the ruined cottage in front of them. Churchill opened her handbag, pulled out two currant buns and handed one of them to Pemberley.

"Well, here we are, the birthplace of the ninth Earl of Middlemop, Humphrey Ridley-Balls. And what a lovely young fellow he is too."

"Even if he bribed Gertie to murder his grandfather?"

"I don't think he could have done that, could he? What an awful thought. Let's consider who else is on our list of suspects. We can't forget about Mrs Surpant, she's still rather suspicious even if she is no longer the beneficiary of the Ridley-Balls fortune. Although it turns out she had nothing to gain from the Earl's death, it's possible that she thought so. The fact that she tried to destroy the will which named Humphrey Ridley-Balls as the beneficiary is certainly suspicious. It doesn't mean that she's a murderer, however it does show that she's not entirely honest."

"And it would have been extremely easy for her to put poison in the Earl's remedy syrup," added Pemberley.

"It would have been exceptionally easy indeed. Now Mr Goldbeam is a funny one as well, although we can't yet establish a motive for him, he was also in the Earl's room at an extremely opportune time, wouldn't you say?"

Both ladies were startled by a terrible honking and flapping noise. A second later, Oswald came dashing over the crumbled wall and leapt up at Pemberley, whimpering.

"Oh poor little Oswald, what happened to you?" She scooped him up and hugged him tightly. Churchill peered behind them towards the river to see a swan's head peering at them.

"It looks like he's upset a swan. Let's move Pembers, it will probably come after us next."

"Oh no! They can break your arms with just a flap of their wings!"

"Can they? Cripes, I didn't realise they were that vicious. Let's move over there, and sit by that old potting shed."

"I want to go home right now!" trembled Pemberley.

"There's no need to go home just yet Pembers, we've got another half hour yet before Mr Speakman returns for us. If we stay away from the swans, we should be quite safe."

The two ladies scurried over to the potting shed and made themselves comfortable in a patch of long grass.

Chapter 32

"Now WHERE WERE we before we were rudely interrupted by the swan?" said Churchill. "Oh, I remember now, we were going over the suspects. I think we've discussed them all now."

"We haven't discussed Tryphena."

"Oh, you know I can't possibly think that Tryphena had something to do with her father's death. But I suppose we must consider it, otherwise you'll start accusing me of treating my friend favourably in all of this. Consider this however, Pembers, if Tryphena was responsible for her father's death, then why would she engage you and I to look into it for her?"

"To make sure that we couldn't consider her as a suspect? Firstly, you're her friend and, secondly, she might hope that because she engaged us to investigate her father's death then we wouldn't suspect her. I'd say it was a clever ruse on both counts."

"I don't think Tryphena thinks like that at all! I think she is an honest person who would not be that conniving and manipulative."

"So why didn't she tell us about the argument by the fountain?"

"Oh Pembers, we've been through this already. She clearly didn't think it was relevant to our investigation. And it probably isn't, if I'm honest with you."

"It's incredibly relevant if she's the murderer. I'd say that she should be our main suspect."

"Main suspect? I find that rather difficult to believe. I agree that we should consider dear Tryphena, however not as the main suspect. I think there are other people who are far more likely. If we're going to consider Tryphena then I'd say that her motive isn't particularly strong. It can only be that she knew her father changed his will regularly and, if she knew that she had been named as a beneficiary in it, then she could have poisoned him before he had the chance to change it again. It's rather a similar motive that we would consider for Mrs Surpant, however when I consider the housekeeper and Tryphena I would say that the housekeeper was far more likely to have done it."

"But did she know she had been named in the codicil?"

"We could ask her."

"But would we get an honest answer?"

"Of course!"

"And what about Cairistiona?" asked Pemberley. "We have to consider that she could have murdered her father."

"Well, I suppose we must consider her. Could she have possibly got into her father's rooms on that afternoon?"

"I should think it's quite likely. She could have found an opportunity in between Gertie, Mr Goldbeam and Mrs Surpant. Just because no one saw her going into his room that afternoon, it doesn't mean that she didn't go there. She knows the house well, and could have sneaked about without being spotted."

"Well there was a little evasiveness about her when we

asked her about that afternoon wasn't there? We know that she was in the drawing room at one point, however she can't have spent the whole afternoon in there can she? She was waylaid by Mr Porge, whatever that means, but I'm sure she had an opportunity to go up to the Earl's room and meddle with his remedy syrup. I don't know what her motive could be, however, unless there is another will or codicil waiting to be uncovered somewhere with her name on it. That seems to be the pattern with this investigation, doesn't it?"

"Neither Cairistiona nor Mr Porge seem to remember what the matter was which waylaid them both in the drawing room," said Pemberley. "I find that strange indeed. They both described it as a household matter, but why can't they recollect exactly what the household matter was?"

"Well I suppose one could argue that the events later that day overtook everything and perhaps rendered such minor incidents rather forgettable," replied Churchill. "However, it is a point worth noting, and I'm not sure how we can ask either of them to remember given that we have spoken to them both and they seem rather reluctant to tell us exactly what they discussed."

"Mr Porge is too secretive for my liking."

"And mine. We need to establish his exact relationship with the basket weavers. And if he's not going to tell us about it directly then we need to find out for ourselves."

"How?"

"Well we know he goes to the pictures in Dorchester every Thursday evening."

"We do."

"Therefore his cottage will be empty."

"Oh no, Mrs Churchill, you think we should break in?"

"Not break in, no, we can access his cottage with a key."

"That's still breaking in."

"No it's not."

"Well, it sounds like breakin' in ter me," came a gravelly voice from the long grass beside them.

Both ladies startled.

"Who is that? Who are you?" demanded Churchill, her heart thudding heavily. "Show yourself!"

A scruffy man with a dirty, wizened face slowly sat up.

"What on earth are you doing there?" she proclaimed.

"What on earth are you doing *there*?" he responded.

"We are here to do some investigating. We're private detectives."

"And I live 'ere," he replied. "You're disturbin' my peace."

"You live here in this ruined cottage?"

"No I live in this old garden. Now if you don't mind I want some peace and quiet now, I've put up with yer ramblin' for long enough."

"Do you know anything about the history of this place?" asked Churchill.

"None. I didn't even realise there was any 'istory."

"Every place has history," replied Pemberley.

"Well if it's got 'istory I ain't interested. All I want is a nice snooze and you're stoppin' me from doing that. I'll say one thing though," he continued. "That's a nice little dog yer've got there."

Pemberley set Oswald down in the grass and the little dog ran up to greet him. Pemberley winced as she watched her pet lick the man's filthy face.

"Is 'e for sale?" he asked.

"No, he absolutely is not!"

Chapter 33

THE TWO LADIES searched for Tryphena at Gripedown
Hall the following day.

"I'm quite sure she won't mind lending us the key for
Mr Porge's cottage," said Churchill as they walked past the
library. "After all, she is the lady of the estate now."

"I still don't think it's a good idea to break into his
cottage," replied Pemberley. "Just the thought of it gives
me the willies."

"No need to suffer from the willies at all, Pembers. Ah,
Mrs Surpant!"

The housekeeper, who'd just emerged from the library,
glared at them.

"I wonder if you could tell us where the lady of the
house is, please?" asked Churchill cheerily.

The housekeeper appeared to wince with pain.

"Is everything all right, Mrs Surpant? I suppose you've
had a rather tumultuous few days. One moment, the
Gripedown estate had been left to you, then it went to
Humphrey and now it's gone to Tryphena."

"Upstairs somewhere," snapped the housekeeper. "And

I trust you have some reliable elastic in your waistband today, Mrs Churchill?" She gave a smirk and went on her way with her nose in the air.

"Oh dear, someone's rather annoyed isn't she?" whispered Churchill to Pemberley. "Mind you, I think I would be too if I were in her position. Imagine having everything one moment and then it all slipping through your fingers the next."

"Oh, I've had that all right."

"When?"

"Too many times."

"For example?"

"Let's go and look for Tryphena upstairs, Mrs Churchill. And don't forget that you must ask her about the argument by the fountain today."

"Oh very well."

A short while later, the two ladies found themselves wondering whether to turn left or right at the top of the staircase.

"It would have been helpful of old Surpant to tell us exactly where Tryphena was, wouldn't it Pembers? She could be just about anywhere. Shall we go left?"

"I think right."

"Right it is then."

They soon found themselves in a long, lonely corridor.

"Look all these closed doors," commented Churchill. "Just think of all the shuttered rooms beyond them."

"A perfect place for ghosts."

"Oh nonsense, Pembers!" Churchill's laugh quickly disappeared in the dingy, echoey corridor.

"I wish we'd brought Oswald with us," whimpered Pemberley. "He stops me feeling scared."

"He's spending precious time with Margery. And besides, you have me here. Is that not reassuring?"

"I can't cuddle you like I cuddle Oswald."

"Well if push really comes to shove, Pembers, I shouldn't mind too much. Now just remember there's nothing to be afraid of. Tryphena will be around here somewhere."

Churchill felt a prickle on the back of her neck as she heard a creak behind them. She glanced behind them.

"What is it?" hissed Pemberley.

"Nothing. Nothing at all, I probably imagined it."

"Imagined *what*?"

"Just a noise. These old places have lots of noises. It's just the structure of the building shifting about."

"That's not supposed to happen!"

"Oh it happens, Pembers. More than you realise." Churchill felt almost convinced herself.

They continued on their way.

"I heard something!" exclaimed Pemberley.

"It's the building shifting."

"It can't be.

Pemberley turned to look behind her and uttered a piercing shriek.

"Good grief, Pembers! What in the—"

Churchill turned too, just in time to witness a figure in light clothing at the far end of the corridor.

"The grey lady!" cried out Pemberley. "Run!" Churchill watched her assistant take off down the corridor then bravely turned to look at the figure again.

But it had vanished.

A cold chill gripped her spine.

"Oh cripes, wait for me, Pembers!"

Churchill ran after Pemberley as fast as her legs would take her. Just as she felt sure she wouldn't be able to catch up, she saw her assistant come to a halt up ahead and emit another shriek. Now she was joined by another figure.

"Another ghost!" cried out Churchill. "Oh good grief, will the good Lord himself please save us!"

But then she saw Pemberley lower her arms and begin conversing with the second apparition. She approached cautiously then recognised the stocky, tweed-attired frame of Tryphena.

"Oh thank goodness!" she called out. "We thought you were… oh, we thought we were done for, didn't we Miss Pemberley?"

"Yes we did."

"You poor things," said Tryphena. "Your imaginations clearly got the better of you!"

She stood by a service staircase which had accounted for her surprise appearance in the corridor.

"We saw the grey lady!" puffed Pemberley.

"You can't have, she's not real," reasoned Tryphena.

"Oh she's *real* all right, she was behind us, wasn't she Mrs Churchill?"

"Well we think she was. We definitely saw something." Churchill gave a shiver. "But perhaps we'd worked ourselves up into a bit of a state."

"There's no doubt you've got worked up about something," said Tryphena. "Shall we go downstairs and have some tea and cake?"

"I've never been in more need of tea and cake. Thank you Tryph. You're such a dear friend."

Chapter 34

"WE MUST CONGRATULATE YOU TRYPH," said Churchill once they were settled in the morning room with refreshments.

"For what?"

"For becoming the lady of the house. The beneficiary of the great Ridley-Balls estate!"

"Oh that! Yes that was quite unexpected. I just happened to find a codicil among Daddy's papers which was dated more recently than the two wills we've found. Quite astonishing isn't it?"

"It certainly is. It makes you wonder if any more wills or cod thingies will be found lying about."

"There are still some papers to go through, so who knows? I haven't caught Mrs Surpant burning anything else in the fire recently."

"Well that's a relief. Do you plan to make any immediate changes to the house? You can always dismiss Mrs Surpant you know."

"Well I suppose I could, however she does do a pretty

good job around here. I shall wait for the outcome of your investigation first, Annabel, and decide from there."

"Well don't let me hold you up. Perhaps you could at least move poor Aunt Nora to the ground floor?"

"I shall have a little chat with her about that. Now I must say that I'm incredibly impressed by your candour Annabel about the whole vicar and petticoat business at the garden party. What made you decide to be so brave and tell all?"

"Between you and me, Tryphena, it was a little ruse I had to pull in order to get my hands on some evidence."

"Golly, really?"

"For another case, not this one. The entire event was fictional but I had to play along. That's detective work for you."

"Indeed, I'm impressed that you risk such public ridicule."

"I laugh in the face of ridicule, Tryph."

"Oh Annabel, how I wish I could be more like you! Now do tell me how your investigation is going. Surely you have a suspect or two by now?"

"We're making gradual progress. In fact, I'm wondering if you could help us with a little something. You mentioned to us a few days ago that you last saw your father when you had a discussion with him about the fountain."

"Yes, that's right. The last time I saw him! I really don't like to think of it like that. It feels like it was only yesterday!"

"Well it was only a short while ago."

"Yes, I realise that, but so much has happened since then."

"Your father's died."

"Yes, isn't it astonishing what such an event does to one's perception of time? Just a few days ago I was speaking to him by the fountain and yet it seems like another era altogether because he's left this world now. Gone. Just like that! In an instant. He was here and... oh, I can't bear it!" She pushed a handkerchief beneath her nose.

"I realise that this is a difficult time for you, Tryphena."

"Oh awful it is, just awful. Never before have I wished that I could turn back the clock. To this time last week! That would be perfect. When Daddy was still here and... oh!"

Churchill waited patiently while her friend blew her nose.

"About the conversation by the fountain," she ventured.

"Oh yes, that."

"We have it on rather good authority, from other members of the household... witnesses we can call them. Witnesses have told us that your conversation with your father was a little more than a conversation."

"What do they mean?"

"They mean that it was, in actual fact, more of an argument. Quite a heated one at that."

"Who told you that?"

"Well I don't think it would be appropriate to share information about witnesses too liberally at the current time, Tryphena."

"But Annabel! You're my friend! Surely you can tell me who's been gossiping?"

"I don't consider this to be mere gossip, Tryphena, it's a little more based on fact than that."

"But you believe them?"

"Are they telling the truth Tryphena?"

Churchill noticed her friend's lower lip wobble. "It was a little more heated than I would have liked."

"So it was an argument rather than a conversation?"

"Well an argument is a form of conversation, isn't it?"

"That's a good point. I don't know." Churchill turned to Pemberley. "What do you say, Miss Pemberley? Is an argument a form of conversation?"

"I suppose so."

"Well there you are, I haven't been misleading you," said Tryphena. "I merely didn't wish to remind myself that I lost my temper a little and now I feel so terribly guilty about it because it was the last time I ever saw my father and I shouted at him!"

She gave another sob.

"What was the argument about?" asked Churchill.

"The cursed fountain! He wanted it repaired and I said it was past repair and a new one was needed. He didn't want to get a new one because the old one was so important to him. I said it had only been a cheap thing which his father had put in and really there must surely be some money to buy a much bigger and better one. He told me that he had no interest in that because he probably wouldn't be, oh!"

She clasped her handkerchief to her face again.

"What is it, Tryphena?"

"Oh, I am sorry." She gave a gulp. "Father didn't want a new fountain because he said it would take too long to have it installed and he might not..." she gave another gulp, "*live* to see it! Oh and how right he was!"

"He didn't live to see it repaired either," responded Pemberley, growing visibly weary of Tryphena's histrionics. Churchill gave her a sharp look.

"No, but..." Tryphena blew her nose again. "If it had been repaired, he would have had an outside chance of seeing it. Oh, what's the use, he's dead now and nothing I can say will change that."

"It would be rather miraculous if it did," said Churchill. "Now, now, Tryphena, you mustn't feel so bad about all this. You felt strongly about the fountain and so did he, arguments are only natural in a family and you weren't to know that you'd never see him again."

Tryphena burst into fresh tears at this reminder. Churchill and Pemberley exchanged a weary glance.

"I don't want you to think I lied, Annabel, because I didn't," continued Tryphena. "I downplayed our argument because I felt so awful about it. I felt such guilt, and still do! Why are you looking at me that way, Annabel?"

"What way?"

"You think I poisoned Daddy, don't you?"

"What? That's absolute nonsense, Tryph, I couldn't even consider such a thing."

"You think I deliberately played down the argument by the fountain and now that I've inherited the estate, you think that I was after it all along!"

"That's not what I think at all, Tryphena, this is a complicated case with a number of suspects."

"Your face says it all, you think it's me!"

"Tryphena, please listen to my words not my face. My face has seen better days but it certainly isn't accusing you of anything."

"I should think the only reason you haven't asked Inspector Mappin to arrest me is because I'm your friend!"

"Now we should stop all this nonsense, it's simply not true."

"Very well." Her expression grew sullen. "But you'd better find the person who did this to Daddy soon, otherwise there really is no point in you working on the case at all."

"Absolutely and we are working on it extremely hard. Now there's something you can assist us with Tryphena."

"Such as what?"

"Are you able to tell us anything about Mr Porge and his sister who we believe is the basket weaver's wife."

"Is she? Well goodness me, I can't believe that at all. How do you know that?"

"Humphrey told us."

"Oh you spoke to him did you?"

"Well we have to speak to everyone, Tryph."

"I see."

"There is a story that your dear father banished the basket weavers and we fear Mr Porge could have felt resentful about it, given his rumoured relationship with them. We've tried speaking to him directly but he denies everything."

"Mr Porge? Resentful? Does that mean he could have…"

"He's a suspect, Tryphena, and we need to do a little more investigating. What we really need is some evidence connecting him to the basket weavers and I'm quite sure that, in that little cottage of his, there must be some correspondence with them."

"Right, well I shall order a search of it. I own the estate now, including his cottage."

"That would be helpful, Tryph. May I suggest, however, that we do it on the quiet? We don't really want him to know that we're going to search his cottage because that would give him the opportunity to hide or destroy anything he doesn't want us to find."

"Very well, what do you propose to do?"

"Well we happen to know that he'll be going to the pictures in Dorchester this evening."

"Of course! As he does every Thursday."

"So Miss Pemberley and I think this evening would be a good time for us to pop down to his cottage and take a little look around. We would need a key, however."

"I don't think Mr Porge is going to take kindly to you looking around his cottage."

"Of course he won't! But he need never know about it."

"You'll leave everything exactly as you find it? So he won't know you've been in there?"

"Absolutely we will."

"Please promise me you will, he'll be very upset if he discovers anything untoward when he returns."

"We promise. Would you mind if we borrow a key?"

"I shall fetch one from Mrs Surpant's office. But on one condition Annabel, please don't breathe a word to anyone that I'm aware of your plan. Now that I'm the lady of the house, I don't want people finding out I've allowed you to search Mr Porge's cottage. There's a danger the staff will become mistrustful of me and I can't have that."

"Absolutely."

"I shall go and fetch the key for you."

"How will you broach the subject with Mrs Surpant?"

"I shall ask for a bundle of keys because I want to do some checks of my own on the estate."

"What an excellent idea, Tryph!"

"Now wait here. And remember, not a word!"

Chapter 35

THAT EVENING, the two ladies visited Mr Porge's cottage in Sparrow's Bottom.

"I don't like this," said Pemberley. "I've had enough scares for one day."

"Scares, Pembers? There's no need to be so jumpy. Mr Porge has gone to Dorchester for the evening and all we need to do is have a little look around his cottage. We'll be no longer than two shakes of a lamb's tail."

Churchill turned the key, the lock gave a satisfying click and the door to the cottage swung open.

It opened into a small front room which was sparsely yet neatly furnished with two easy chairs, a table and a dresser. The low evening sun shone a bright ray on the far wall.

"Now where do you suppose he keeps his letters?" whispered Churchill.

"In a writing desk?"

"Where's his writing desk?"

"I don't know."

They stepped through the front room to a room at the

back which had a small stove in it, a sink and a dining table with two chairs.

"Very modest accommodation," said Churchill. "What you'd expect from a man like Mr Porge. No sign of a writing desk though. Shall we try upstairs?"

"Must we? Can't we just leave now? There's nothing here."

"We must try upstairs, Pembers." They returned to the front room from where a narrow staircase led to the upper floor. They tip-toed up it and Churchill winced when one of the stairs creaked.

"I don't know why I'm so worried about making a noise," she said. "There's nobody here."

"I hope nobody's here," hissed Pemberley. "How would we explain ourselves?"

"We'll just behave like two confused old women, that usually works. Just craft an expression of bewilderment on your face, Pembers, and you'll be immediately let off the hook."

The staircase brought them to a small landing with two doors.

"Two bedrooms I suppose," said Churchill, pushing open one of the doors.

"I don't want to go into Mr Porge's bedroom!" protested Pemberley in a loud whisper.

"Well I can't say it's at the top of my list of places I want to visit either, Pembers, but needs must."

They pushed open the first door and found that it opened into a small box room.

The second door opened into a simply furnished bedroom with a bed, wardrobe, chest of drawers and washstand.

Churchill walked over to the chest of drawers. "Surely

we will find some correspondence stashed in here, what do you think, Pembers?"

"I don't like rifling through people's drawers."

"Neither do I, but it has to be done if we're going to solve this case. Now come along, let's have a look."

"I dread to think what we might find."

"Oh come along, Pembers. At the very worst, it will be Mr Porge's undergarments."

"Exactly! And those are the last things I want to see."

"There's no need to be squeamish about a gentleman's undergarments. I suppose I have the stomach for them after being married for forty years. Perhaps it's a little too much for me to expect a spinster such as yourself to tolerate them."

"I have no tolerance whatsoever, if you don't mind, Mrs Churchill, I'll let you look through the drawers." Pemberley glanced out of the window at the setting sun.

"Very well."

Churchill began opening the drawers and investigating the contents of each one. "Some vests in this one," she commented. "Socks in here…"

"I don't want to know!" protested Pemberley.

"Sock suspenders. I wonder if they've been repaired with the dodgy elastic? Mr Porge could have been one of the complainants couldn't he?"

"Are there any letters?"

"No, but I've found his long johns."

"Ugh!"

"Calm down, Pembers. I'm happy to report they appear to be perfectly clean."

"It's not cleanliness I'm worried about, it's the mere thought…"

"Now this drawer here looks interesting, I appear to have happened upon some personal effects."

"Letters?"

"Too early to say yet, but certainly some papers."

"Can't we hurry, Mrs Churchill? I feel terribly nervous in Mr Porge's bedroom."

"Why? No one could possibly discover us here, Pembers. The projector reel has probably only this minute begun turning at the Dorchester picture house. We have hours of time on our hands. Now then, let's have a look. These look like letters…"

As Churchill examined the papers in her hand, Pemberley glanced out of the window again and saw two figures approaching the cottage.

"Oh heck!" she exclaimed. "Quick, Mrs Churchill, someone's coming!"

"Who?"

She glanced quickly out of the window again. "Mr Porge! He's come back! And he's got someone with him! A woman!"

"Oh good grief, are you sure you're not imagining things, Pembers?"

"Absolutely sure. Oh golly, they can't find us here. We must hide!"

A bolt of panic shot through Churchill's bosom. She shoved the papers into her handbag and slammed the drawer shut.

"But where, Pembers, where?"

She scanned the little room, her eyes falling on the wardrobe. In an instant, both ladies dashed towards it, flung open the doors and attempted to step inside. Their entry was thwarted by a large leather trunk. Churchill bent down and began to haul it out.

"You can't touch it!" hissed Pemberley. "He'll notice it's been moved!"

"Well what then?"

"We'll have to hide somewhere else!"

"Such as where?"

"Under the bed!"

Churchill prayed that there was nothing else beneath the bed as she clumsily prostrated herself on the floor and rolled beneath it. Her chest and stomach wedged beneath the frame as she wiggled herself out of view. Pemberley lay next to her, her breath quick and shallow.

"What if he looks beneath here?" hissed Pemberley.

"We're doomed, that's what." Churchill's heart pounded heavily in her chest. "I don't understand," she continued in hushed tones. "I thought he was at the pictures!"

"Clearly he wasn't."

"I realise that now."

They heard a man's voice and a woman's voice down-stairs. Churchill was gripped with tension as she stared at the bottom of Mr Porge's mattress just inches from her nose.

"They're going to come up here!" hissed Pemberley. "I just know it!"

"It would be most inappropriate if they did."

"I'm quite sure they couldn't care whether it was appropriate or not. What if they do?"

"We'll worry about that when the time comes, Pembers. Now try not to get too flustered, we'll think of a plan."

"Try not to get *too flustered*?" protested Pemberley. "But we're lying beneath his bed! How on earth are we going to get out of here without him noticing?"

"We can wait until he's asleep, Pembers?"

"*Asleep?*"

"Yes, he's an early riser isn't he? I'm sure he'll be

retiring for the night soon. Only an hour or two to wait, I'd wager."

"I can't wait an hour or two. I can't bear another five minutes staring at the bottom of his bed. I can't bear it at all!"

"All we need to do is distract ourselves, Pembers, and the time will soon pass. Now then, who's he with?"

"I don't know."

"You didn't recognise her?"

"She's wearing a hat, from the angle of the upstairs window, the brim was covering her face."

"Was she tall, short, fat, thin?"

"In between all of those things."

"I wonder who on earth she could be. He clearly lied about going to the pictures which suggests to me that he didn't want anyone to know he was meeting her. It's an illicit liaison. I'm rather annoyed we didn't uncover it sooner, our investigative process should have revealed it to us before now."

"Well I'd say that our investigative process has well and truly revealed it now, wouldn't you, Mrs Churchill? And I'd be pleased about it if only we weren't stuck beneath his bed."

Peals of laughter rose up from the room beneath them.

"Good grief, Pembers. Whoever she is must be quite special if she's managed to raise a laugh from old misery Porge. I've never seen him so much as crack a smile, have you?"

"No. But then he's always on duty when we see him."

"We visited him here once though, didn't we? We didn't manage to make him laugh then."

"We were questioning him about a murder, the opportunities for a laugh were few and far between."

"I suppose so. Oh I wonder who that woman is. Who

can she be, Pembers? It wasn't, perchance, Mrs Thonnings was it?"

"No."

"How do you know? You say you didn't see her face."

"She wasn't wearing the sort of thing Mrs Thonnings wears."

"A floral tea dress or a cheap blouse you mean?"

"Exactly."

"So what was she wearing?"

"Just an ordinary dress of some sort. Not particularly bright or patterned, so ordinary that I can't recall any distinguishing features. Mind you, I only looked out of the window quickly."

Another peal of laughter interrupted them and then they heard footsteps on the stairs.

"Oh no!" whispered Pemberley. "He's going to find us here!"

"Perhaps not," reassured Churchill, her heart pounding again. "Perhaps he's going to retire for the night and then we can creep out while he's asleep."

"I don't think he is," replied Pemberley. "I think she's coming up with him!"

Churchill listened and, sure enough, she could hear both voices on the stairs.

"But she can't come up here!" she whispered. "It's not allowed!"

"I don't think they care!"

The two ladies fell silent as they heard laughter on the landing.

"I expect the vicar is still recovering," said Mr Porge. "Can you imagine the sight? It would have put me quite off my sandwiches."

"Oh Charlie, you are a scream!" laughed the woman.

Churchill did her best to ignore the flush of shame as

she realised what the couple were laughing about. Instead, she concentrated on the woman's voice; she felt sure that she'd heard it somewhere before. But to whom did it belong?

"I aim to please," chuckled Mr Porge in a low tone Churchill hadn't heard him use before.

She felt her heart sink as the bedroom door opened and two pairs of feet appeared next to the bed. Mr Porge wore a well-polished pair of brogues and the lady's shoes were of brown leather with decorative punch holes and a strap and brass buckle.

She turned to Pemberley who had a look of horror etched on her face.

"Now put your drink down and make yourself comfy, darling," said Mr Porge.

Churchill now felt a mask of terror on her own face. She turned to Pemberley again and the two ladies stared at each other, eyes and mouths agape.

"Don't mind if I do," purred the woman. The mattress squeaked loudly above the two ladies' faces as the woman's weight sank onto the bed, her feet disappearing from view. A surge of panic rushed through Churchill's body, from her feet to her throat. She managed to resist the urge to cry out, but the urge to leave the room was beginning to take hold.

She stole a glance at her assistant who now appeared to be weeping with her eyes screwed shut.

"Oh Charlie, I think you need to oil your bed springs," said the woman as the discarded shoes were tossed onto the floor.

"What, now?"

"No, not now. You silly old teddy bear. Come and lie beside me."

As the bed squeaked a second time, Churchill knew that she couldn't bear another moment.

"Stop!" she called out, desperately trying to wiggle her way out from beneath the bed. "Just stop this minute, let me out!"

The loudest scream she had ever heard erupted in the room.

In an instant Pemberley scrambled out. More screams ensued and Churchill wiggled furiously to free herself from beneath the bed.

"What are you doing here?" cried out Mr Porge. "What's going on?"

"N-n-n-nothing," came Pemberley's faltering response.

As Mr Porge shouted in reply, Churchill tried desperately to free herself so that she could explain everything.

But it was no use. She was stuck fast.

Chapter 36

"THIRTY-FIVE YEARS of policing and I thought I'd seen it all," said Inspector Mappin, with a shake of his head. "I can't even begin to comprehend, Mrs Churchill, what your explanation can be for this."

Churchill and Pemberley sat in Mr Porge's front room with the inspector, Mr Porge and Cairistiona Vigors-Slipcote. Churchill gave a sigh and tried to decide what should take precedent in her mind: the humiliation of being discovered beneath the butler's bed or the revelation that Mr Porge was having a liaison with Mrs Vigors-Slipcote.

Cairistiona avoided everyone's gaze and stared sullenly at her fidgeting hands.

"We couldn't find Oswald," Churchill began, "and there were reports that he'd been seen in the window of Mr Porge's cottage."

"What?" exclaimed the butler.

"Yes we found it difficult to believe too," said Churchill. "Anyway, my assistant and I came here to investigate and found you weren't at home. Terribly worried for the welfare of your furniture, Oswald does have a tendency to chew chair legs you see, we decided that it was a matter of urgency that we retrieved him from your home."

"Did you see Oswald in the property before you broke in?" asked Inspector Mappin.

"No, I can't confess that we did. And we didn't break in, we used a key."

"And where did you get the key from?"

"We borrowed it from the house."

"With Mrs Surpant's permission then?"

"Well we couldn't find her either but we felt quite sure that she would have given her blessing if we had asked her as there was an urgent need to remove the dog from the cottage and we felt sure that she would agree."

"I don't understand," said Mr Porge. "How did the dog even get into my home?"

"We don't know, he has a knack for such things. He really is quite clever."

"And where's the dog now?" asked the inspector.

"We don't know, we couldn't find him in here so perhaps he wasn't here after all."

"You say there were reports he was seen in the window," said Inspector Mappin. "Which window?"

"To be honest with you, Inspector, a particular window wasn't specified."

"And who said they'd seen him in the window?"

"Can you remember who it was, Pembers?" Churchill turned to her assistant and wished that she could be a little more resourceful and helpful at times like this.

"I can't remember," came the reply.

"Surely you must be able to remember who told you?" queried Mr Porge.

"Well there was a general flurry at the time," replied Churchill. "We noticed he was missing and we panicked and asked an awful lot of people in a short space of time if anyone had seen him and someone, obviously we forget who now, said they'd seen Oswald in the window of your cottage. That was all they said, they didn't explain which window. And, in fact, once they mentioned that, we didn't stick around to hear any more because we were so intent on rushing down here to fetch him."

"But you had time to grab the key first?" asked the inspector.

"Erm, no. Once we realised that Mr Porge wasn't at home, we had to dash up to the house to fetch the key and then dash back again."

"And you let yourself into Mr Porge's cottage."

"Yes."

Inspector Mappin scratched his head and looked at the notes he'd been making. "Your story has some vague plausibility about it, Mrs Churchill, but it falls down in the failure to explain how you, and Miss Pemberley, ended up beneath Mr Porge's bed."

"Well having looked downstairs for Oswald, we thought he might have gone upstairs. Therefore we went upstairs to have a look. Then we heard the key in the door downstairs and, quite frankly, we panicked and decided to hide ourselves."

"But why couldn't you just have explained to me that you had broken into my home to look for your dog?" asked Mr Porge.

Churchill now wished this was the approach she had taken. "The bright lights of hindsight really do shine harshly on one's actions, don't you find Mr Porge? I can explain it no better than for the fact that we momentarily lost our heads, especially when we noticed that you had a companion."

Mr Porge gave an awkward cough. "I don't see what that has to do with anything."

"It's quite apparent that you and Mrs Vigors-Slipcote wouldn't wish to be seen together."

"So to save our blushes you decided to spring a surprise from beneath my own bed?"

"That was never quite the intention, Mr Porge. I do apologise for startling you."

"What was the intention, Mrs Churchill?" asked Inspector Mappin.

"We thought that we could wait under the bed until Mr Porge was asleep and then creep out of the house."

A knock at the door heralded the arrival of Tryphena. She gave Churchill and Pemberley a regretful stare, as if they were her children who'd been caught stealing apples from the orchard.

"What are you doing here, Carrie?" she asked.

A silence ensued then Inspector Mappin began an explanation of the evening's events. "This is your cottage, Miss Ridley-Balls," he said at the end, "would you like charges to be pressed? I should add that this isn't the first time Mrs Churchill has been caught trespassing."

"Actually it's my cottage," said Mr Porge. "Don't I get to decide?"

"It belongs to the Gripedown estate," replied Tryphena. "And I don't think there's any need for you to be here, Inspector, in fact I'm not sure why you were called in the first place."

"They terrified me!" cried out Cairistiona.

"Well you're hardly blameless yourself, Carrie!" retorted Tryphena. "Carrying on like that with the *butler* for goodness sake! You should be thoroughly ashamed of yourself!"

"If no further action is to be taken, then can I please leave?" asked Inspector Mappin. "I'm actually supposed to be off-duty and Mrs Mappin will take a dim view if my supper's left to get cold."

"Of course, Inspector, I'm sorry you were troubled with this incident this evening. Annabel? May I have a word with you and Miss Pemberley outside?"

Churchill didn't like the stern expression on her friend's face. She and her assistant sullenly rose from their seats and followed Tryphena outside.

"I've decided something, Annabel," she said with a sigh. "With much regret, I don't think it's right for you to be investigating this case any more."

"This was all a silly mistake, Tryph, we thought Porge was at the pictures! And so did you, didn't you?"

"Yes I'd assumed he was telling the truth about that and now I really understand what's been going on. But to get stuck under Mr Porge's bed? It's shameful, Annabel. And on top of the incident at the garden party with the vicar and your petticoats."

"That didn't happen."

"But everyone thinks it did! It was on the cover of the local newspaper, Annabel! I'm sorry, you were once a dear friend and now it appears that you're little more than a laughing stock."

Churchill opened her mouth to argue, then resolutely closed it.

"I see. Well I do apologise, Tryphena, if I've embarrassed you."

"You've not embarrassed *me*, Annabel, you've embarrassed yourself."

"Fine. Well let's be on our way, Miss Pemberley."

"Would you like me to call you a taxi?" asked Tryphena.

"No need. We can walk."

"All that way?" protested Pemberley.

"It will give us time to talk, my trusty assistant. After all, we were so incredibly close to catching the suspect, weren't we?"

The two ladies sadly made their way up the lane from Sparrow's Bottom.

"So I suppose this is it, Pembers, the end of the road for our investigation. Why couldn't Tryphena explain to Mr Porge that she gave permission for us to search his cottage? She was covering her own back and that's most unfair. There really was no need for her to get rid of us in that manner, I'm sure that if we'd been allowed to continue, we would have found out who was behind it."

"It's unjust."

"It most certainly is."

"And for what it's worth, Mrs Churchill, I don't think you're a laughing stock."

"Well thank you, Pembers, that means a great deal to me."

Oswald cantered across the lawn to them with Margery and the two ladies greeted them.

"If you ask me, I think Tryphena became unnerved when we probed her about the argument by the fountain," said Pemberley. "Maybe our enquiries were too close for comfort?"

"I think you could be right. All this business about me being an embarrassment is just misdirection. She was probably worried that our suspicions were falling on her and she found the perfect excuse to get rid of us. But we'll show her, Pembers!"

"Will we? How?"

"I don't know yet, but I'll make sure of it. I don't take these things lying down."

"Not even when you're stuck under a bed?"

"Absolutely not." They paused in front of Gripedown

Hall. "Now let's have a quick look at the papers I managed to pull out of Mr Porge's drawer," said Churchill. "Roger and Dora Pipwaite were the names of the basket weavers. You have a quick look through these, Pembers," she said, thrusting a bunch of papers at her assistant. "And I'll have a look through these."

"What if someone sees us?"

"There's no one around at the moment. Just have a quick look through and see if there's any correspondence from Dora Pipwaite."

The two ladies hastily examined the letters in their hands.

"Nothing here with that name on," responded Pemberley.

"Oh that's a shame, nothing here either."

"There's a postcard though. From Bognor Regis."

"And?"

"It's a nice beach, isn't it? With some grand looking hotels on the seafront too." Pemberley turned the postcard over. "And it's signed 'Roger and Dora'."

Churchill felt a warm sense of satisfaction wash over her.

"I knew it, Pembers! Now we have proof! Quick, let's get them back in my handbag."

Churchill smugly closed the clasp and glanced up at the house.

"Oh look there's Aunt Nora in the window up there, give her a wave Pembers."

The old lady acknowledged them with a wave of her own.

"So what do we do about the postcard?" Pemberley asked as they began walking down the driveway.

"That's a good question. We're no longer on the case so I have no idea what to do with it."

"Oh dear, it all seems like a waste of time then."

"It does rather, doesn't it? Perhaps we'll think of something. For the time being, we shall have to concentrate our efforts on proving that Mrs Bouton wrote those poison elastic letters."

Chapter 37

THE FOLLOWING MORNING, Churchill and Pemberley headed up the cobbled high street towards lavender-fronted Boutons et Rubans.

"Now then Pembers," said Churchill, "can you remember our plan?"

"Yes. I distract Mrs Bouton with an important question while you sneak behind the counter and have a rummage around in her wastepaper basket."

"Excellent. I think it's a foolproof idea which will ensure that we can find a scrap of paper with an example of Mrs Bouton's handwriting on it."

Pemberley asked Oswald to wait outside the shop while the two ladies stepped into the perfumed interior. The multitude of colourful trimmings greeted them once again and a soothing tune played on the gramophone.

"It's even busier than last time we were here," observed Churchill. "It's just what we need. With everyone distracted by each other, it will be easy to execute our plan without Mrs Bouton spotting what we're up to."

"Are you sure?" asked Pemberley. "I'm getting quite

nervous now. It all sounded like a good idea when we were planning it, but now that we're here I'm rather nervous it could go horribly wrong."

"What could go horribly wrong?" asked Churchill.

"The whole plan. I keep remembering what happened in Mr Porge's bedroom."

"Forget all about that unfortunate incident, this is very different altogether. You just do the distracting and I'll do the rest."

"Oh hello there again ladies," said Mrs Bouton cheerfully, her thick, golden curls bouncing on her shoulders. "You don't seem to be able to stay away. What can I help you with this time?"

"Oh I'm looking for some…" Pemberley cast Churchill a panicked glance.

"Some of that fancy new ribbon everyone's buying," said Churchill.

"I know the one," replied Mrs Bouton with a smile, "it's been very popular this week, in fact some of the colours have sold out altogether. Would you like to have a look at what I have available?"

Pemberley and Churchill exchanged a knowing glance before Pemberley followed Mrs Bouton into the maze of display stands. Once she felt sure the haberdasher was a good distance away, Churchill edged towards the counter and peered behind it.

She had just spotted the wastepaper basket when she heard a voice behind her.

"Hello Mrs Churchill!"

She turned to see Mrs Harris with her fair hair and protruding teeth. "How are you?"

Churchill forced a smile to hide her frustration that the moment of opportunity was slipping by.

"I'm very well thank you Mrs Harris. Now if you don't

mind I'm on the lookout for something in particular, we don't have long in this shop because we're very busy."

"Of course Mrs Churchill, have you recovered?"

"From what?"

"The public shame. You know... the skirt and the vicar."

"Quite recovered thank you," she snapped. "Now if you don't mind, I must get on with what I'm looking for."

"Yes of course." Mrs Harris gave an awkward smile and swiftly moved away.

Churchill moved closer to the counter and stood in a position where she'd be able to quickly dart behind it. After a visual sweep of the shop, she stepped behind the counter and ducked down so that she could no longer be seen.

Now on hands and knees, she began shuffling towards the wastepaper basket, dragging her handbag which was looped around her wrist. A few cardboard boxes had to be navigated around and the little table, on which the gramophone sat, appeared rather rickety.

A few moments later, Churchill reached the wastepaper basket. She held her breath as she delved in. Rummaging as quickly as she could, she closed her hand on an apple core. She had to suppress a gasp of revulsion before rummaging around some more.

The sound of the gramophone was loud in her ears and she felt an increasing panic as time ticked by. Surely she would be spotted at any moment? Working quickly, Churchill pulled several balls of paper from the wastepaper basket and shoved them into her handbag. There was no time to examine them closely.

Once she'd decided that she had enough discarded paper, Churchill discovered there wasn't sufficient room behind the counter to turn around on her hands and knees. Cautiously she began to reverse out of the space but voices close to the counter made her startle.

She had to move fast.

Churchill shuffled backwards as fast as her knees would allow.

Then her foot hit something and the gramophone stopped playing. The sickening realisation that she'd knocked the needle off the gramophone record began to engulf her. There was nothing more to do other than get out from behind the counter.

"Mrs Churchill?" came Mrs Bouton's voice. "Are you all right?"

"Oh dear, it looks like she's had another one of her falls," said Pemberley's voice.

"That's right, I did!" she called out, relieved at Pemberley's moment of quick-thinking. "Yet another fall! Silly old me. Could someone help me up please?"

Chapter 38

A SHORT WHILE later the two ladies were sat at Churchill's desk with tea and chocolate biscuits. The balled up scraps of paper from Mrs Bouton's wastepaper basket had been smoothed flat and laid out for them to examine.

"Notes on various ribbons and buttons and pieces of fabric and whatnot," commented Churchill. "I've no doubt they're a good example of Mrs Bouton's handwriting."

"Which looks nothing like the handwriting on the letter which was sent to Smithy Miggins.

"Indeed. Most unfortunate."

The handwriting on the papers extracted from Mrs Bouton's wastepaper basket was elegant and looping, quite unlike the sharply slanted handwriting which was on the letter which had been sent to Smithy Miggins.

"The handwriting on the letter to the newspaper is very convincing and I wouldn't say that it has been forged at all," continued Pemberley, "it looks like someone's natural hand. And the same can also be said of the hand-writing on the scraps of paper here. The pen is quite different too, the ink in the newspaper letter is black and blue on the scraps of paper."

"Well, I should think different coloured inks doesn't mean that Mrs Bouton didn't write the letter. But the handwriting is wildly different, isn't it?" Churchill gave a sigh. "Our only hope is that Mrs Bouton is extremely good at disguising her handwriting. Other than that, I should say that these were written by entirely different people."

She sat back in her chair and helped herself to a fourth chocolate biscuit.

"I fear we're not getting anywhere with any of our investigations, Pembers. Tryphena has thrown us off her case and now we're getting nowhere with the poison elastic letters. We really are adrift now. Where did it all go wrong? We had such a good run of solving cases and now we find ourselves completely stuck. I'm going to have to sit back as hapless Inspector Mappin makes a hash of the murder case. In fact, the case may never be solved at all which would be awful. Tryphena may even come to regret getting rid of us, don't you think Pembers?"

"Not if she's the murderer."

"You know, Pembers, it's not a bad suggestion. It's all worked out rather well for her hasn't it? She probably doesn't need us now that she's inherited the estate. Perhaps it doesn't matter to her now to even find out who murdered her father. If it was her, then she doesn't want anyone to find out does she? Perhaps this was all one big ruse from the very beginning? Perhaps she only befriended me so that she could then hire me and then dismiss me as part of an elaborate illusion that the case was being properly investigated? What a tragedy. The Earl's death remains unsolved and Tryphena is getting away with the spoils."

Churchill took a gulp of tea and felt even more sad about the whole sorry affair.

Footsteps sounded on the stairs and Mrs Thonnings bustled into the room.

"Oh dear, you both look thoroughly miserable," she commented. "Has somebody died?"

"No one since the eighth Earl of Middlemop," replied Churchill. "However we are a little fed up because our investigations have all ground to a halt."

"Even the investigation into the letters which were sent to the newspaper? Have you not been able to prove it was Mrs Bouton yet?"

"Not yet I'm afraid Mrs Thonnings, and I don't think we can find any evidence at all that she sent those letters. Look, here we have the letter which was sent to the *Compton Poppleford Gazette* by the mystery writer. And here we have some examples of Mrs Bouton's handwriting, they look completely different."

Mrs Thonnings looked closely at the papers. "I see what you mean."

"So I'm rather tired of it all now and would like to go and take a little holiday by the sea."

"Bognor Regis looks nice," said Pemberley. "On a postcard."

"Oh it is nice," replied Mrs Thonnings. "I had a lovely honeymoon there with my third husband."

"*Third?*"

"I think I can hear someone coming up your stairs," said Mrs Thonnings.

The office door flung open and in strode the bulky form of Mrs Higginbath. Churchill was sure she heard Pemberley give a slight whimper. Even Oswald cowered behind a filing cabinet

"Good afternoon Mrs Higginbath, what can we help you with?" asked Churchill.

"*Notable Rock Formations in Shropshire*, that's what," fumed the librarian.

"I-I've got it with me," stammered Pemberley. "It's just here in my d-drawer somewhere, I think I can find it."

"May I ask what it's doing in your drawer instead of sitting on a shelf in the library?" asked Mrs Higginbath.

"I was planning to bring it back later today, I'm terribly sorry Mrs Higginbath, it's kept slipping my mind we've been ever so busy you see."

"If you're too busy to return books to the library Miss Pemberley then you shouldn't borrow them in the first place."

"I realise that Mrs Higginbath and I'm so terribly sorry about it, I don't believe I've had an overdue library book for about thirteen years."

"That's all very well and good Miss Pemberley, however this transgression will mean a black mark against your name. Once you have three black marks, you will lose your reading ticket."

"Oh Mrs Higginbath, you are a horrible bully!" exploded Churchill. "You heard my assistant just now. Thirteen years! For *thirteen years* she has returned her library books on time. Now we have one which is merely a week overdue and you're marching in here scolding her and treating her like a little schoolgirl. It's a disgrace and you shouldn't be allowed to be a librarian."

Mrs Higginbath turned to her, hands on hips. "And what do you think would happen if everybody neglected to return their library books on time, Mrs Churchill?"

"Well I shouldn't think the sky would fall in on our heads, Mrs Higginbath. Now please fetch the book from Miss Pemberley and leave us in peace. You're disturbing us."

"Well it makes a change from you disturbing me in the library," retorted the librarian.

Pemberley sheepishly handed the book to Mrs Higginbath.

"Thank you," she snapped. "And do you have a penny for the fine?"

Pemberley rummaged through her handbag. "Yes it's just here."

She handed Mrs Higginbath the coin.

"Thank you, Miss Pemberley. Don't let it happen again."

"Boo," said Mrs Thonnings, once the librarian's footsteps had faded away. "What a villain."

"Indeed, Mrs Thonnings. Haven't you got a shop to be getting back to?"

"Now I'm really riled, Pembers," fumed Churchill, after Mrs Thonnings had left. "That Mrs Higginbath enrages me. To have her marching into our office like that and bullying you in that way! We're having a bad week. Our cases have come to a juddering halt and now we're doomed to sit here feeling sorry for ourselves forever."

"Oh goodness it's not that bad is it?" replied Pemberley. "I wouldn't allow Mrs Higginbath to annoy you like that, I was in the wrong for not returning my library book on time. Let's forget about her for now and decide what we're going to do. We can surely do something? Where there's a will, there's a way."

"Exactly the sort of thing I like to say. Pembers, I must say that you're quite good at helping one feel better about things."

"Oh I don't know about that. It's nothing really."

"Don't be so dismissive of your talents, Pembers, there's a very good reason why you're my trusty assistant."

"Really, what is it?"

"Very funny. There you go, you see. You make me laugh."

"Not intentionally."

"Even funnier!"

"I don't understand."

"Now then," Churchill picked up her pen. "All is not lost. We're going to find out who put cyanide in the Earl's remedy syrup. The trouble is, we're not allowed to carry out any more investigations so we need to work with what we have."

"But do we have enough?"

"It will have to be enough."

"And what if we get it wrong?"

"There's always that risk I suppose. But what else can we do? Now I know it's easy to laugh at the supernatural goings-on in that place, Pembers, but having been spooked out by such things ourselves, I think we also need to take them a little more seriously."

"The ghosts?"

"Yes, and although some say they're not real, we know that they influence the place all the same. Now I saw something quite intriguing yesterday, did you?"

Pemberley considered this for a moment.

"No."

"Well I did and I think you did too. Allow me to explain."

Chapter 39

"So what do you think, Pembers?" asked Churchill, after she had finished her explanation.

"I think you're enormously clever, Mrs Churchill, and absolutely everyone should hear your theory about the Earl's death," replied Pemberley. "But there's a problem."

"What?"

"We've been thrown off the case. Tryphena doesn't want us involved any more. She even called you an embarrassment."

"I remember what she called me thank you, Pembers, I don't need reminding. However there's someone I think can help us."

"Who?"

"Inspector Mappin."

"The inspector? Surely he's the last person who'll help us?"

"Not if I tell him who murdered the Earl. He'll be more than happy to get his handcuffs ready. I'll telephone him now and, with a bit of luck, he'll help put the plan into place."

Chapter 40

"WE'LL SLIP into the room at the last moment," said Churchill to Pemberley as they arrived at Gripedown Hall the following afternoon.

"And what if Tryphena tells us to get lost?"

"Well we must do what we can. Hopefully Inspector Mappin has done a good job of rallying the troops for us."

"I'm amazed that he agreed to it."

"I'm not, Pembers. The man follows the path of least resistance. If someone else has worked out the case for him, then all he has to do is bask in the glory of making an arrest at the end of it."

The two ladies heard the buzz of voices as they walked down the corridor to the drawing room. Inside, the furniture had been arranged as it had at Mr Verney's reading of the will. Today the top table was occupied by Inspector Mappin and two police constables. Churchill and Pemberley sidled to the back of the room, trying not to be noticed.

Tryphena noticed them, however, and glared.

Churchill formed her mouth into a noiseless whistle and fixed her eyes on the faded curtains.

"She's staring at us," whispered Pemberley.

"I know, I know. If we ignore her for long enough, she'll hopefully lose interest."

Inspector Mappin made a point of looking important at the top table as he leafed through papers and consulted with his constables in a low voice.

"He's enjoying this, isn't he Pembers? And this is why it wasn't too difficult to convince him to arrange this little get-together."

Churchill surveyed the room and saw that Cairistiona was present, along with Mr Porge and Mrs Surpant. Gertie sat next to Humphrey Ridley-Balls and Inspector Mappin had somehow convinced Mr Goldbeam to attend too. Aunt Nora dozed in her bath chair and a number of village onlookers had turned up including Mrs Thonnings and Mrs Higginbath.

"I think all the important people are here," whispered Churchill. "Time for Mappin to get on with it."

A few moments later, one of the constables stood up and blew his whistle. Everyone was startled into silence.

"Thank you Dawson," said Inspector Mappin, getting to his feet. "A little louder than I'd anticipated but it certainly got everyone's attention. Now then, I've gathered you all here this afternoon to inform you of the outcome of the investigation into the murder of the eighth Earl of Middlemop, Richard Aubrey Ridley-Balls. As you're all aware, he was tragically murdered ten days ago after a person, or persons, unknown placed cyanide into his bottle of Dr Crumpot's Remedy Syrup. My colleagues and I have worked relentlessly on this case and we sincerely hope now that the Ridley-Balls family will find some comfort in the announcement we will be making this afternoon."

"Bravo, Inspector," called out Tryphena, leading a round of applause. Mappin gave an appreciative nod as everyone clapped.

"Why are they clapping for *him*?" whispered Pemberley. "He's done diddly-squat as far as I can see."

"I suppose it's because he's the local constabulary and the strong arm of the law."

"No one ever claps for us."

"We don't require applause to flatter our egos, Pembers. We merely do our job because it's the just and right thing to do."

"And now, without further ado, I shall hand over to a lady who is much better accustomed to public speaking than myself," said the inspector. "Mrs Churchill."

Churchill felt all eyes on her as she and Pemberley made their way to the front of the room. She half-expected Tryphena to protest at her presence but everyone remained reassuringly quiet. Inspector Mappin took his seat and Churchill pulled a bunch of papers from her handbag.

"Good afternoon," she said to the room. "Thank you for coming. Thank you, Inspector Mappin, for your introduction. Now I'll get on with it, shall I?"

She arranged her papers and felt the weight of everyone's expectation on her, not unlike the audience in a music hall waiting to be impressed by the first act.

"Now the facts of the case are as follows," she began. "On the day of his death, the Earl of Middlemop had his usual afternoon nap in his rooms after lunch. He woke at three and had a conversation with his daughter, Tryphena Ridley-Balls, by the fountain at about four o'clock." She pointed to the fountain beyond the windows. "We've established that there was some debate about whether to repair or replace the fountain and it became rather heated. In fact it was an argument which Miss Ridley-Balls was reluctant to admit to. Why did she not admit this was a heated argument? Was it because she felt guilty about arguing with her father on the day of his death? Or maybe it was because the argument had something to do with his death?"

"It had nothing to do with it!" exclaimed Tryphena. "We've been over this, Annabel!"

"The heated argument was witnessed by Cairistiona Vigors-Slipcote from this very room," continued Churchill. "However, despite witnessing her sister and father's distress, she didn't intervene or even speak to either of them afterwards. The excuse she gave was that she was waylaid by the butler and valet, Mr Charles Porge, about a household matter. Neither she nor Mr Porge have elaborated on what this household matter was and it may be relevant to add that the two have been conducting an extra-marital affair."

She paused to allow for a few gasps.

"It's not relevant at all!" protested Mr Porge.

Cairistiona's head was bowed, as if in shame.

"The housekeeper, Mrs Susannah Surpant, attended to the Earl in the library after the argument with his daughter Miss Ridley-Balls," continued Churchill. "He appeared quite angry about it and Mrs Surpant arranged for Gertie to bring the Earl's afternoon tea to the library. At six o'clock, the Earl retired to his bedroom to eat his supper. The observant ones among you will notice that the Earl was therefore away from his rooms from the hour of three o'clock until six o'clock."

"I noticed that," chipped in Mrs Thonnings.

"Good. Now this means there was a three hour window of opportunity for someone to visit the Earl's bathroom and put cyanide into his dyspepsia medicine. So who went into his rooms during that time? Well first of all we have the handyman, Mr Vincent Goldbeam, who was called in to unblock the Earl's chimney. How do we know the chimney was blocked? We know this because the maid, Miss Gertie Pinks, had tried to light the fire in the Earl's room. When the chimney wouldn't draw, she notified Mrs Surpant who then called in Mr Goldbeam. We therefore know that Mr Goldbeam, Gertie and Mrs Surpant were in the Earl's rooms during the time he was downstairs.

"Another person who was in the Earl's rooms that day was, naturally, the butler and valet, Mr Porge. Gertie has informed us that Mr Porge was with the Earl when she took his supper up at six o'clock. This was the usual routine of course. After assisting the Earl with retiring for the night, Mr Porge finished his duties at around seven o'clock.

"So we have four people who, we can say with certainty, were in the Earl's rooms that day. Perhaps there was an opportunity for someone else to sneak in and put the poison in his remedy syrup? We shall see. However, I think it's important to establish what the motive was for the Earl's murder. He was ninety-nine years old, why on earth would someone wish to murder him?"

"That's what I've always wondered," called out Mrs Higginbath. "Was it a mistake?"

"The answer could lie in the Earl's propensity for drawing up wills and codicils to amend his wills," continued Churchill. "No one has admitted the Earl discussed his inheritance with them and that could be because, by making such an admission, they could reveal themselves as a suspect. Did someone persuade him to leave everything to them in his will? Did that person murder him before he could write them out of it again?"

"Mrs Surpant," said Tryphena.

"What nonsense!" cried out the housekeeper. "We

discussed this and I think it's quite obvious that I would never do such a thing! I've been deeply upset by my employer's death and wouldn't dream of poisoning the poor old man. He did mention that he had put a little something for me in his will, but I certainly had no intention of murdering him just so that I could receive it. And besides, I have been vindicated by the fact that more wills and codicils were made afterwards."

"Yes, you didn't quite manage to destroy *all* of them in the fire did you, Mrs Surpant?" retorted Tryphena.

"I had no idea I was throwing a will into the fire! I thought they were old papers."

"What an enormous fib!" exclaimed Cairistiona. "Papa shoved that will up his chimney! When you saw what it was, you hid it and then tried to destroy it!"

"You have no evidence for that whatsoever!" responded the housekeeper.

"Ladies, ladies…" interrupted Inspector Mappin. "That's enough. Please allow Mrs Churchill to proceed."

"Thank you Inspector. I turn now to the ninth Earl of Middlemop." Churchill smiled at the handsome man sat in front of her. "A man with a complicated past."

"Well I wouldn't say it was particularly complicated, Mrs Churchill," he replied with a grin.

"You were named in one of the Earl's wills," she continued. "And omitted from others. Any idea why?"

"None whatsoever. That was Grandpapa for you. A contrary old fellow if ever there was one."

"There's a rumour that your parents were Roger and Dora Pipwaite, the basket weavers."

"Merely a rumour."

"Of course. Although you are missing the family ears."

"Family ears?" stated Tryphena. "What on earth do you mean by that, Annabel?"

Churchill moved swiftly on. "Perhaps no one will ever know for certain whether there's any truth behind the rumours of Humphrey Ridley-Balls's parentage, however the eighth Earl thought enough of the rumours that he persuaded Mr and Mrs Pipwaite to leave. A decision which no doubt angered Mr Porge."

"Why?" asked Mrs Higginbath.

"Mrs Pipwaite is Mr Porge's sister."

"Nonsense!" he snapped.

"Yes you can keep denying it all you like Mr Porge. However, my assistant and I found this." She held up the postcard from Bognor Regis. "The date is a mere four years ago and I shall read it out to you, 'Dear Charles. Lovely weather and good breakfasts at the hotel. Roger and Dora.'"

The butler let out a dry laugh. "That proves nothing!"

"I agree that it doesn't prove a great deal, Mr Porge, but are you really going to insist on denying that Mrs Dora Pipwaite is your sister?"

"I don't know." He glanced around him sullenly. "It depends."

"On what?"

"On whether you're going to accuse me of something."

"Well I think you have a motive for murdering the Earl, Mr Porge. I think you were angry that your employer forced your sister and her husband to move away. You bore him resentment. Am I right?"

"I'm not admitting to anything like that."

"No, I expect you'll protect yourself until the very bitter end, Mr Porge."

"And anyway, you stole that postcard from my home!"

"I borrowed it. Here, you can have it back."

Churchill held the postcard out to him but he didn't move.

"All right then, I'll leave it on the table here and you can collect it at your leisure, Mr Porge."

"So is he the murderer?" called out Mrs Thonnings.

"All in good time," replied Churchill. "I would like to talk about ghosts now."

Chapter 41

"Ghosts?" laughed Tryphena. "I've told you before that the ghosts in this house aren't real, Annabel!"

"Have you told that to Mrs Surpant?"

"She knows they're not real too!"

Churchill turned to the housekeeper whose face was now a little paler than before. "Do you believe in the ghosts in this house, Mrs Surpant?" she asked.

"No."

"But didn't you see something on the evening the Earl died?"

"That's right, she did," said Mr Porge. "When Gertie summoned us after she'd found the Earl deceased, Mrs Surpant and I both dashed upstairs. She got there before me, because of my leg. And when I encountered her in the corridor outside the Earl's rooms, her face was as white as a sheet. She told me that she'd just seen the grey lady. Now I'm as much of a sceptic about these things as the next man, but that's what she told me."

"Well I don't like to admit to it," said the housekeeper. "But I did think I saw something that evening in the corridor. My mind was quite affected by the Earl's death of course. It may have been nothing. However, it's always been said that the grey lady appears at the time when somebody dies."

"Was she close to you, or far away?" asked Churchill, mindful of her own recent experience.

"She was at the far end of the corridor, in the distance."

"This gives me the shivers!" called out Mrs Thonnings.

"Gertie," said Churchill. "You were in the Earl's room a few times on the day he died."

"Yes," stammered the maid. "But I was only doing my job, Mrs Churchill! I found him dead like that, I didn't do nothin'!"

"You were responsible for keeping an eye on the Earl's remedy syrup and providing him with new bottles when needed."

Gertie nodded.

"For some reason you collected the supply of his medicine a week earlier than usual."

"Because Mrs Surpant told me to."

"Interesting. You had plenty of opportunities, did you not, for tampering with his medicine?"

"But I never did!"

"Perhaps someone asked you to put something in his medicine? Perhaps you didn't realise that what you were putting in there was harmful? There are a number of people who could have asked you to put something in the Earl's remedy syrup. Mrs Surpant, for example. Perhaps Miss Ridley-Balls or Mrs Vigors-Slipcote?"

This comment elicited protestations from the ladies mentioned.

"Or even Humphrey Ridley-Balls?" suggested Churchill.

"Now there's a thought!" chimed Tryphena, glaring at the man.

"Perhaps you didn't put anything in the Earl's medicine, Gertie," said Churchill. "Perhaps Mr Goldbeam did so, instead?"

"Me?" he asked incredulously. "Why would I do that?"

"Perhaps someone asked you to do it, Mr Goldbeam? After all, you were alone in the Earl's rooms for a while that day. Perhaps someone blocked the chimney on purpose so that you could be called out and pressed into action?"

The handyman glanced nervously around at the staring faces. "No one asked me to do nothing of the sort!"

A general murmur now spread through the room.

"Am I being accused of something now or not?" asked the handyman. "I better not be arrested! All I did was unblock a chimney!"

Churchill cleared her throat and the room quietened again.

"Has anyone considered that the grey lady could be a real person?" she queried. "I ask, because, shortly after I was told by Miss Ridley-Balls the other evening that my services were no longer required, my assistant and I walked past this house. We looked up at the windows and saw something odd."

"What?" asked Tryphena.

"The grey lady. And it wasn't the first time we'd seen her. I'm going to suggest to you now that the grey lady is a real person. The grey lady is not a ghost. She is alive and well, and very old. She is the Earl's sister."

Everyone turned to stare at the old lady dozing obliviously in her bath chair.

"Aunt Nora?" queried Cairistiona.

"But she's stuck in a bath chair," said Tryphena.

"Sometimes she's stuck in her bath chair on the top storey," replied Churchill. "But when Miss Pemberley and I saw her at the window she wasn't on the top storey at all. She was on the first storey. Quite close to the Earl's rooms in fact."

"How did she get there?"

"She must have walked. And she must have been walking when Miss Pemberley and I caught a glimpse of her at the far end of the corridor a few days ago. It must have also been what she was doing when Mrs Surpant saw her shortly after the Earl's death."

"That was Mrs Ponsonby-Staithes?" queried Mrs Surpant.

"Mrs Nellie Hallwick," said Churchill. "You're Mrs Ponsonby-Staithes's nurse. Can you tell us when she supposedly lost the use of her legs?"

"It was about three months ago."

"A gradual loss of use or quite sudden?" asked Churchill.

"Very sudden."

"Interesting. I suggest that Mrs Ponsonby-Staithes took a long time to prepare for this murder and planned it well. She decided that nobody could suspect her if she were an invalid completely confined to the upper storey of the house. Immediately she would be discounted as a suspect in her brother's death if everyone believed that she could no longer get down the stairs by herself and had to have someone to help her at all times. She continued this ruse for about three months so that everybody believed that she was incapable of walking about the house. I'm not sure whether she purposefully decided to act like a ghost, but, she was aware of the supernatural rumours and maybe thought she could spook people for fun."

"I refuse to believe it!" protested Nellie.

"Were you with Mrs Ponsonby-Staithes for the entire time on the day the Earl was murdered?" asked Churchill.

"Not the entire time. She has a nap every afternoon, just as her brother did, and during that time I usually see to some other chores."

"So she was left alone for a period of time that afternoon?"

"She would have been, yes. But she certainly wouldn't have gone off and poisoned her brother, that would have been most unlike her!"

"Whether it was unlike her or not," replied Churchill, "is there a possibility that she could have visited his rooms between the hours of three o'clock and six o'clock?"

"Yes."

"You were not with her for the entire time between three and six?"

"No."

"And what about eight o'clock?"

"What do you mean?"

"Mrs Surpant claimed to have seen the grey lady at eight o'clock, shortly after the Earl was discovered dead."

"Mrs Ponsonby-Staithes is in bed by then."

"Was she in bed at that time on that evening?"

"She would have been, yes, because I always put her to bed at seven o'clock."

"A bit early isn't it?" commented Mr Goldbeam. "I'm only getting started at that time of the evening."

"Probably because you're not ninety-seven," responded Churchill. "Now then, Mrs Hallwick, is it possible that Mrs Ponsonby-Staithes could have been up and about at eight o'clock in the evening without you realising?"

"She could have been, yes. But I don't believe she can walk, she's been in this chair for three months!"

"May I ask where you were at eight o'clock that evening?"

"I was in the servants' kitchen."

"I can vouch for that," said Mrs Surpant.

"Good. And now for the cyanide," said Churchill. "Mrs Ponsonby-Staithes mentioned to my assistant and I that there had been a problem with rats in her rooms."

"Yes that's correct," replied the nurse.

"And where was the poison stored?"

"In a little cupboard at the end of the corridor."

"Could Mrs Ponsonby-Staithes have accessed the cupboard?"

"Yes."

The room fell silent as everyone now considered the possibility that the dozing old lady could have poisoned her brother.

"Aunt Nora a poisoner?" called out Tryphena. "Have you lost your mind, Annabel? It's absolutely impossible! How can you accuse an old lady who is confined to a bath chair of actually being able to walk? She's just a dear old lady, she wouldn't even comprehend doing such a thing! And to suggest that, on top of all this, she actually murdered her own brother is quite astonishing! I think this is a desperate attempt for you to try and name the murderer, Mrs Churchill, the fact is you have no idea who did this!"

The thought didn't appear to rest easily with Inspector Mappin either. He shifted about in his chair and had a perplexed scowl on his face.

"Can we wake up Mrs Ponsonby-Staithes and put this to her?" he asked the nurse.

"We can try," she replied. "Although she can be a little grumpy after she wakes."

"I think she should hear the accusation which has been levelled against her," said the inspector.

The room appeared to hold its breath as the nurse nudged Aunt Nora awake.

The old lady's eyes opened and she surveyed everyone's faces. "Are you not finished here yet?" she asked. "Why are you all looking at me?"

Inspector Mappin got to his feet.

"This could be an uncomfortable moment," whispered one constable to the other.

The inspector cleared his throat. "Mrs Ponsonby-Staithes," he began. "There's been the rather... well, I'm not sure what to call it really... preposterous suggestion that you actually have the use of your legs after all."

A faint look of bemusement appeared on her lined face.

"And..." he gave another cough. "That you may have crept down to your brother's rooms and put cyanide into his bottle of Dr Crumpot's Remedy Syrup."

A grin now broke out onto the lady's face. "Finally you got there, Inspector! Clever you."

"You don't deny it?"

"No. What's the point?"

"So you admit that you murdered your brother?"

"Yes I do."

"Oh nonsense, Aunt Nora!" called out Tryphena. "You couldn't have possibly done such a thing!"

"Why not? Because I'm old?"

"No, I didn't say that."

"But you suggested it."

Inspector Mappin rubbed his brow. "If you admit to the murder," he said. "Then can you explain why you did it?"

Aunt Nora got to her feet and walked over to the table. Everyone stared open mouthed.

"He annoyed me for too long," she responded. "Ninety-seven years to be exact. I'd had enough of his griping and complaining and general misery."

"How could you?" cried out Cairistiona, leaping to her feet. "What a cruel, cruel, thing to do. Poor old dear Papa!"

"That's enough of that," replied the old lady, "you didn't have to spend your time in the same house as him. I did! And for many years too. Sixty-two to be exact. I'd just had enough."

"You began planning this three months ago?" queried Inspector Mappin. "When you decided to pretend you couldn't walk?"

"I began planning it before then. I decided no one could ever suspect me if I couldn't move around of my own accord. It was a pain being confined to that chair thing for so long but it fooled everyone except you, Inspector."

"In fact, it was Mrs Churchill you didn't fool."

"Oh! The detective lady?" She turned to Churchill and grinned. "I used to be a lady detective once. I told you that, didn't I?"

"You certainly did," replied Churchill.

"I suppose I get arrested now?" said Aunt Nora.

"You don't have to admit to anything, Mrs Ponsonby-Staithes," said the nurse, taking her arm. "You're perfectly entitled to deny it and find a lawyer."

"Oh what's the point? I'm ninety-seven, Nellie. What are they actually going to do with me?"

Chapter 42

"I suppose I should apologise, Annabel," said Tryphena when she visited the office the following morning. "I shouldn't have dismissed you from the case and you're not an embarrassment at all. Quite the opposite in fact. I'm impressed you went on to solve it despite all my silliness."

"Thank you, Tryph."

"I felt wounded that you would consider me a suspect, but that was foolish of me. And as for that incident beneath Mr Porge's bed, I considered it a terrible lapse of your judgment at the time but I suppose we can laugh about it now."

"Possibly. Would you like a slice of cherry cake?"

"I would love one, thank you Annabel. And as for dear Aunt Nora…" she shook her head in disbelief. "I can only think she went doolally. She and Daddy didn't get on, but I didn't realise it was quite that bad."

"Where is she now?"

"Still in the cell at the police station. I think Inspector Mappin feels terribly bad about confining her. He's got

Nellie down there to attend to her and, quite frankly, Aunt Nora appears to be enjoying the attention and change of scene. To be honest with you, I don't think she's left Gripedown for about fifteen years."

"Gripedown which is now yours, Tryphena. Once the recent events are behind you, perhaps you may grow to enjoy being lady of the manor?"

"Oh," she gave a sigh. "I don't suppose you've heard then."

"Heard what?"

"Another codicil was found."

"Oh no, not another one?"

"Yes, I think poor Daddy was also going a little doolally during those last few months."

"So who benefits from the latest codicil?"

"Margery."

"The *dog*?"

"Yes, Margery the dog." Tryphena gave a weary laugh. "I have no idea how that's going to work."

"Did you hear that, Oswald?" said Pemberley. "Your little lady friend is a member of the landed gentry!"

"It makes no odds to him, Miss Pemberley. They're just dogs."

"He's excited, Mrs Churchill! I can tell by his face!"

A brief knock at the door was followed by Mrs Thonnings bustling into the room.

"Oh I'm sorry!" she glanced at the visitor. "I didn't realise you were busy."

"We're not busy," said Tryphena. "Just eating cherry cake."

"Oh. Is there some spare?"

"There certainly is, Mrs Thonnings," said Churchill. "What's that in your hand?"

"A piece of paper."

"I can see that. Have you brought it here to show us?"

"I have." She paused and her face coloured a little. "Actually, it's a love letter."

"Cripes, well I don't think you want to be sharing such private sentiments with us, Mrs Thonnings."

"Well I wouldn't normally. But it's the handwriting you see. It looks familiar."

"To the poison elastic letter?"

"Yes."

Churchill opened her drawer, rummaged about and pulled out the letter which had been sent to Smithy Miggins.

"Come on then, Mrs Thonnings, let's have it."

She placed the two pieces of paper next to each other on her desk.

"By golly, you're right!" she exclaimed. "Come and look at this, Miss Pemberley!"

Her assistant hurried over to her desk and surveyed the letters.

"They're written by the same person!" Pemberley clapped her hands together in glee, then began reading from the love letter, "'The moment I saw you in the drawing room at Gripedown Hall, I knew I'd made a mistake. I was sulking, I did some bad things and I'm sorry. I hope you forgive me.' Oh... what does that say? Oh dear, I'm not sure I want to read the next bit."

"There's no need to read it," said Mrs Thonnings. "It's just a silly letter."

"Who wants you to forgive them?" asked Churchill. "Who's Vinnie?"

"Vincent," said Pemberley. "Surely?"

"Yes!" The realisation dawned on Churchill. "Vincent Goldbeam! He wrote the poison elastic letters as an act of revenge after you ended the relationship, Mrs Thonnings?"

"Yes," replied the haberdasher. "And he feels terribly bad about it. He says he's going to make it up to me by helping me spruce up my shop. So it turns out that it was nothing to do with Mrs Bouton after all!"

"Well that's wonderful," replied Churchill. "It would have been helpful if Mr Goldbeam had made his confession sooner, it would have saved us a lot of trouble and public humiliation. But all's well that ends well I suppose. Goodness, I've just noticed the last line of this letter, you'd better have it back, Mrs Thonnings."

"Oh I don't want it. Don't you need to keep it as evidence?"

"No. I shall dispose of both letters in my wastepaper bin."

"Two cases solved," said Pemberley.

"Clever ladies," said Tryphena. "Well I should be going." She got to her feet. "I need to stock up on a few things while I'm in the village. One of my tweed skirts requires some repair so I shall pay a visit to that delightful new haberdashery. What's it called again? A lovely French name I seem to recall."

"I have no idea," responded Churchill, her jaw clenched with unease.

"Oh you don't want to be going there Miss Ridley-Balls," said Mrs Thonnings.

"Why not?"

"I hear the *Compton Poppleford Gazette* has received some letters of complaint about that place."

Mrs Thonnings gave Churchill a surreptitious wink.

"Oh Mrs Thonnings…" said Churchill. "Surely, you haven't…?"

The haberdasher winked again. "Buttons pinging off apparently," she added. "The letters should be printed in the next day or two, you'll get the full story then. To stay on the safe side, Miss Ridley-Balls, why not pay a visit to my shop instead? I can do you a nice little offer on tweed skirt repair kits."

"Can you really?"

"Yes, I'm just heading there now. Care to accompany me?"

"Well there we have it, Pembers," said Churchill, after the two ladies had left. "Perhaps Mrs Thonnings and Tryphena will become firm friends now. And fancy the entire Gripedown Estate being left to a dog! Have you ever heard anything so ridiculous?"

"I don't think it's ridiculous at all."

"You don't?"

"After the week we've just had, Mrs Churchill, I think it's the most sensible thing I've heard in a long time."

The End

Thank You

~

Thank you for reading *The Poisoned Peer*, I really hope you enjoyed it!

Would you like to know when I release new books? Here are some ways to stay updated:

- Join my mailing list and receive the short story *A Troublesome Case*: emilyorgan.com/a-troublesome-case
- Like my Facebook page: facebook.com/emilyorganwriter
- Follow me on Goodreads: goodreads.com/emily_organ
- Follow me on BookBub: bookbub.com/authors/emily-organ
- View my other books here: emilyorgan.com

And if you have a moment, I would be very grateful if you would leave a quick review of *The Poisoned Peer* online. Honest reviews of my books help other readers discover them too!

Get a free short mystery

~

Want more of Churchill & Pemberley? Get a copy of my free short mystery *A Troublesome Case* and sit down to enjoy a thirty minute read.

Churchill and Pemberley are on the train home from a shopping trip when they're caught up with a theft from a suitcase. Inspector Mappin accuses them of stealing the valuables, but in an unusual twist of fate the elderly sleuths are forced to come to his aid!

Visit my website to claim your FREE copy:
emilyorgan.com/a-troublesome-case

Or scan this code:

Get a free short mystery

The Augusta Peel Series

~

Meet Augusta Peel, an amateur sleuth with a mysterious past.

She's a middle-aged book repairer who chaperones young ladies and minds other people's pets in her spare time. But there's more to Augusta than meets the eye.

Detective Inspector Fisher of Scotland Yard was well acquainted with Augusta during the war. In 1920s London, no one wishes to discuss those times but he decides Augusta can be relied upon when a tricky murder case comes his way.

Death in Soho is a 1920s cozy mystery set in London in 1921. Featuring actual and fictional locations, the story takes place in colourful Soho and bookish Bloomsbury. A read for fans of page-turning, light mysteries with historical detail!

Find out more here: emilyorgan.com/augusta-peel

The Penny Green Series

Also by Emily Organ. Escape to 1880s London! A page-turning historical mystery series.

As one of the first female reporters on 1880s Fleet Street, plucky Penny Green has her work cut out. Whether it's investigating the mysterious death of a friend or reporting on a serial killer in the slums, Penny must rely on her wits and determination to discover the truth.

Fortunately she can rely on the help of Inspector James Blakely of Scotland Yard, but will their relationship remain professional?

Find out more here: emilyorgan.com/penny-green-victorian-mystery-series